IMMORTAL MERI

BURIED

EMMA SHELFORD

BURIED

Kinglet Books
Victoria BC, Canada

Cover design by Deranged Doctor Designs

ISBN: 978-1989677162 (print)
ISBN: 978-1989677094 (ebook)

www.emmashelford.com

First edition: March 2019

DEDICATION

For the cast and crew of BBC's Merlin*: your unsatisfying final episode to a beautiful series turned the wheels of my imagination. Thank you.*

CHAPTER I

I soar far above the city of Vancouver on feathered wings. The wind is brisk and ruffles my pinion feathers, and the late summer sun warms my back. I shriek my delight to the blue skies, and a crow far below me looks up in alarm.

Too soon, the roof of the auto body repair shop appears as a tiny postage stamp on the ground. I tuck my wings together and plummet in a steep dive toward a cluster of trees near the shop. The trees will give me cover for my transformation, not that anyone would believe their eyes if they saw it.

I open my wings at the last moment and flap heavily between branches to the ground. The grass is dry and brown here, in need of autumn rains that are still months away. The trees surround a tiny ravine with the riverbed clay dry and cracked. Nobody ever comes down here. It's a perfect place to revert to my human form.

Crackling grass between my talons disappears once my human foot is ensconced in a sock and shoe, and the roar of traffic, almost deafening to my avian ears, reduces to a dull hum. I shake my head to feel the movement of my body once more, and my hands pat down my shirt. It's time to pick up my car, finally fixed from the hailstorm of weeks ago.

There's a deep groaning noise from somewhere deep below me. I whirl on the spot to find the source, but nothing appears out of the ordinary. The groan resonates again, and the hairs on my neck stand up. That's not a noise made by human, animal, or machine. It is from the Earth.

Faster than I can move, a yawning hole splits open at my feet. Dry dirt clods crumble into the dark fissure as it opens. I jump into the air and desperately fumble with my lauvan to transform into a falcon once more, but I can't catch the right

1

strands in time. My body plummets into the newly created sinkhole.

I brush against waving threads of earth lauvan as I fall. They slip through my fingers but slow me enough that when I reach the bottom of the crack, it is not so jarring. My heart pounds, and my breath comes in sharp gasps, but now that I'm not falling, I can stand on shaking legs and look around.

My ankles are deep in loose dirt, although firm soil under the soles of my shoes reassures me that I will not fall farther. The crack is twice my height, but only as wide as my shoulders, so it's a tight squeeze. An earthworm at the level of my eyes wriggles free of its earthen confinement and falls to my feet. It smells of mold and damp and growing roots. Somehow, the scent relaxes me, and my brain tries to unravel this mystery.

Why did a sinkhole appear in the middle of Vancouver? Even if this city were prone to them, which it isn't, the conditions aren't right. And what are the chances that a random sinkhole appears directly below my feet and swallows me whole?

Very low chances, indeed.

As if in response to this thought, earth lauvan sinuously float from the dirt walls to wrap around mine. I expect this and hold still to allow the connection. If there is anything I learned from almost getting drowned by water spirits, it's that I shouldn't put up a fight with spirits who only want to talk. And what else is this sinkhole, this crack in the ground that didn't leave a scratch on me, if not a very large appeal for my attention?

My lauvan relax and allow the earth strands to intertwine with them. Soon, some of the strands coalesce into the vague form of a head and torso. A voice emerges from the region of the mouth.

"Merlin. You are here." The voice is low and gravelly and speaks slowly. I raise an eyebrow.

"Hard not to be, since you dropped me in this hole. Did you have a reason, or does it simply amuse you?"

The voice speaks without acknowledging my cheek.

"We did not want you to flee when we spoke. The connection is clearest deep in our element, and you cannot escape easily. We can speak to you now."

"Yes, about that. I have a lot of questions. This seems like a great time to clear some things up. Your water counterparts were not very forthcoming."

"Water is slippery and cannot be pinned down, but earth is unmoving. We will answer your questions if we can. If we cannot, we will never yield."

That isn't a great start to a conversation. What do they want from me?

"Why are we talking?"

"Do you know of others who are like you? The successor wishes to know."

"Other teachers? Other handsome men? Other people who were around when the Magna Carta was signed?"

There is a pause in which I almost detect a small sigh. Have I goaded the earth spirits too much? It's strange, but whereas I felt only anxiety and fear in the presence of the water spirits, with these earth spirits I am far more comfortable. Perhaps I am getting used to dealing with spirits, and they don't faze me in the same way.

"Others who can see the threads of the world. What do you call them?"

"Lauvan," I say. "But your words are far more poetic. I know of no others who can see lauvan. I have never met anyone else, and I doubt they exist."

"The world is a large place, and there are many people in

3

it," the voice says in a musing tone. "Doubtless they do not advertise their abilities. That is all we wished to know. Goodbye for the moment, Merlin."

"Wait," I say with a mix of alarm and command filling my voice. "I want to ask you a few things. How do you know my name?"

"We have found out many things about you but cannot tell you the source."

"Fine. It doesn't matter." I run my hand through my hair while I think of another question, but there's only one way I'll get the answers I want.

"Can I talk to the successor now?"

"After the ceremony to bring us each within a human body. Once that is complete, the successor will speak with you. Until then, it is not possible."

I growl audibly. What's the point of speaking to the spirits, of having a connection to this world beyond our own, if I can't get answers from it? It's time I try a little harder.

My fingers grasp the nearest earth lauvan that surround my own and squeeze tightly. My eyes close and I send my thoughts into the strands, just as I do when I travel through the lauvan cables in my mind's eye. I want to see if I can find spirits in the strands.

There is nothing to see, but my mind feels a presence. It's hard and solid, a block in my way, and I can't move past it. Instead, I press against it. Flashes of sensation flit through my brain—the roar of a landslide, the unbelievable pressure of a diamond underground, the heat of molten magma at the earth's core—and they fill every corner of my mind. My heart beats in a thunderous counterpoint. The sensations are so foreign, and yet fill me with pleasure and comfort all at once, as if my body finally feels what it has been missing.

It lasts only a moment, then the solid presence in the lauvan flees beyond my reach. It leaves an emptiness that I don't know how to fill. I open my eyes to a wall of dirt and unreactive earth lauvan. The spirit must have left. Did I startle it? Was it not expecting me to show such abilities? To date, I haven't been able to show much strength in the face of the spirits, so they might not have anticipated that I would fight back one day.

I must have connected with the spirit. Did I see its memories, or whatever passes for memories in the spirit world?

But still, the spirits refuse contact with this mysterious successor, and the only way they will allow it is after Potestas members invite spirits to possess their bodies. I am very tempted to let Potestas complete their ceremony, if only so I can have my questions answered by this successor. I don't know what the spirits intend in their human hosts. Could it be that bad? As for the Potestas members that will lose their bodies to these parasites, well, it is their choice. How far do I have to save people from themselves?

I must try. They really don't know what they're doing and what the spirits truly intend.

CHAPTER II

It's only been two days since I came back from my sea journey with March Feynman to find the grail in a shipwreck off the coast, the grail that will allow Potestas to bring the spirits to Earth, but it's time I stopped procrastinating. I need to hide the grail somewhere Potestas will never find it.

This sinkhole will accomplish that task. I try to turn every situation to my advantage, and today is no exception. The grail is hidden in my satchel, and barring keeping it on my person always, I need a hiding place for it. My apartment is out, as Potestas knows where it is and how to get in. Now that I understand how powerful their spirit connections are, even before the ceremony, I don't trust any barrier I can devise. No, the grail must be hidden somewhere obscure.

I take the grail out of my bag and admire its enameled bowl before I place it near my feet. If I can get out of here and fill the hole, the grail will be gone for good. Well, nothing is ever gone for good, but gone for long enough that Potestas won't be able to profit from it.

I look around the sinkhole and analyze it for exit strategies. The walls are sheer and crumbling, and the grassy lip of the hole is too far away to reach, even with outstretched arms. I dig my toe into the side for a foothold and am rewarded with a shoe full of dirt. I could transform back into a falcon, but there isn't enough room for my wings to spread. Tree roots poke through the soil at intervals above my head, and I touch one. It's thick and sturdy, with rough root hairs along its length.

It's time to see how much upper arm strength I've retained. I don't swing a sword every day, now, but my body doesn't forget very quickly. I grasp the root and haul myself up, then snatch at another root higher up. Up and over, my hands grab roots above my head until grass tickles my fingertips. The edge crumbles until I hold onto a large rock embedded in the ground and drag my body over the edge.

I lay on the grass, winded and sweaty. When I catch my breath, I stand and survey the damage. My clothes are covered with dirt, and my fingers encounter huge clods of the stuff in my hair when I tousle it clean. My fingers run through the earth lauvan that accompany the dirt and attempt to pluck them away to remove the soil, but it's very difficult to separate my own brown strands from the earth ones by sight. I try for a few minutes, then give up and dust my clothes off the best I can. I still look like I crawled out of a dustbowl, but it will have to do.

I don't often close gaping holes in the Earth, but I'd better figure it out before my hiding spot is noticed. I walk around the edge of the sinkhole, careful not to fall in, and bend down so my fingers can grasp any loose earth lauvan that they can touch. Once my circuit is complete, my hands are full of the silvery-brown strands. Slowly, relentlessly, I pull.

The earth groans and shudders. I step back to avoid falling when the walls of the sinkhole churn and crumble. Dust fills the air and I press my nose and mouth into the crook of my arm to breathe through my shirt. A minute later, all that is left of the hole is a rough patch of bare dirt and a cloud of dust that drifts away in the light breeze.

It's a short walk to the shop, and besides a suspicious look from the repairman that lasts until I produce identification, the car pickup goes smoothly. I slide into the low seat of my Lotus with a contented sigh then point the nose toward my apartment.

Voices emerge from my apartment door when I open it. Jen stands in front of the couch with an open duffel bag at her feet. Alejandro tosses clothes and shoes inside. Jen looks up at me with a smile.

"Hi, Merry. What happened to you?" She eyes my dirty clothes with puzzlement.

"I hid the grail. Potestas will keep their grubby hands off it now." I look at the duffel bag. "What's going on?"

"Packing," Alejandro says. He lobs a rolled sock into the bag like a basketball. "I can move into my new place today."

"Lucky it's furnished," says Jen. "You really don't have much. I bought a few things to spruce up the place. They're in my car."

Alejandro beams at Jen, and their lauvan connection shivers. Another two strands connect them at the words. I suppress a smile. They are in the sweet beginnings of a relationship, and it's heartwarming to see.

Then I consider what Alejandro's move means to me, and my mood lowers. The apartment will be very quiet when he is gone. I've been alone too much in my life to enjoy the sensation. Alejandro must notice, because he turns to me.

"Don't worry, Merlo. I'll be back more than you want me to be. Your fridge always has beer in it."

I laugh.

"That's how to win friends and influence people."

"And you'll have more freedom," Alejandro says. He grins at me. "I'm sure Minnie won't mind."

"Don't forget stuff in the bathroom, Alejandro," says Jen.

He moves down the hall, and I reflect on their relationship and my own with Minnie. Theirs is innocent in a way that mine can never be. I've seen too much, done too much, lost too much to dwell in sweet bliss. But Minnie and I are comfortable in a way that doesn't happen very often. Are we too comfortable? I wonder. I don't want to travel down that road, the road that Jen and Alejandro are barreling down. I don't want to love right now. I don't want to fall apart, to splinter into pieces.

But it's only a fling, a short dalliance with a lovely woman. I'm sure that's all it is on my part. Next time I see Minnie, I will examine her lauvan closely to make sure she feels the same. I don't want to cause her more hurt than is necessary. She deserves that consideration.

"Anything new with you?" I ask Jen to banish my thoughts.

"I visited my dad at his office yesterday. He just sold off his security company that he bought before I was born." Jen's father is CEO of a multinational corporation, with footholds in numerous industries. It doesn't surprise me that they own their own security company. "It doesn't matter, really, except that my favorite guard is gone. Barty used to give me candies whenever I visited as a kid and tell me stories of his childhood in Hungary. And now he's gone." Jen shrugs. "It's a little sad I didn't get to say goodbye. The sale happened a few weeks ago, but I haven't visited my dad at work in a while."

"Perhaps Barty is guarding a celebrity, or a treasure chest of gold doubloons," I say to lighten Jen's mood. "Keep Barty in your memory and imagine he's doing more interesting things than guarding the front desk of an office building."

Jen purses her lips in thought.

"Maybe security for a newly discovered tomb in Egypt. Or Aztec gold in the Yucatan."

"Exactly."

"In other news, I have more questions for you."

"You always do." For the past three days, ever since she found out about my history, Jen has been asking me questions. She'll have enough to write a book soon, at the rate she's collecting information.

"Where were you in eighteen eighty-three, when Krakatoa exploded?"

Krakatoa, or Krakatau as it was known to the Indonesians at the time, was the largest volcanic eruption in written history.

"I'd settled in Perth, Australia, for a time. I was part of the team that built the first telegraph line there, and it was such an odd little place, with such fantastic scenery, that I stayed for a while. The Western Australian gold rush provided extra entertainment. But Krakatoa—the incredible explosion that day, no one knew what the noise could possibly be. It was a few days later that the news finally made it to Perth."

Jen shakes her head, as if to force the answer to make sense.

"Have you ever ridden an elephant?"

"Really? The answer is yes, several times throughout my life. There are plenty of your contemporaries who could say the same."

"I like elephants," she says in defense. "Okay. Have you ever killed anyone?"

"Yes."

Jen appears taken aback by my quick response.

"Over your whole life, how many people have you killed?"

"Far too many to count," I answer with easy assurance.

Jen's lauvan freeze at my response, and her face tightens. Then she gives a forced laugh.

"That was a nonchalant answer."

I shrug.

"It's true. Most of history was far bloodier than in present-day North America. Wherever there are humans together, there will be conflict. And I lived by my sword as a mercenary, as a raider, or as a knight, for much of my life."

Jen nods slowly, but her lauvan stay taut. I break the short silence.

"No more questions?"

"Not today." Jen pastes on a fake smile. "Maybe later. I'll get Alejandro settled into his new place."

She walks toward the bathroom where Alejandro packs his toiletries. I am left wondering about Jen's reaction. Surely, she would have guessed my answer? She has taken enough history classes to know that the past was often brutal. Does she see me in a different light now?

CHAPTER III

Minnie slides into the passenger's seat.

"Hi," she says, then leans toward me. I greet her waiting lips with a quick kiss then start the engine.

"Where to, my lady?"

"Can we stop by the farmer's market in Burnaby? I'd love some fresh fruit."

"Your wish is my command."

I accelerate away from the curb, but at the sight of Minnie's whitened knuckles on her purse I slow down to a more moderate pace. She would trust me more if she knew of my long experience behind the wheel, but I don't tell short-term lovers of my past. That would be far too risky. I'll simply have to slow down for now.

"How are you feeling lately?" Minnie asks. She winces. "Sorry, that was a therapist question, wasn't it? I do try to keep work at work. But I still want to know your answer."

"I'm well, thanks." I laugh. "Was that what you were looking for?"

"I was more curious about your issue from last week. Have you heard any voices lately?"

I was overcome by the voices of water spirits yelling in my head during one of our recent dates. I was too shaken up to hide it from Minnie, and she's been after me to see a professional to help with the voices. I can't tell her they were spirits.

"I haven't heard any voices that I haven't wanted to hear."

"Good." Minnie leans back with satisfaction. She likely thinks I've only been hearing real voices, human voices from physical bodies. I meant that now I want to hear what the spirits have to say.

Conversation is easy between us, as always, and it's a quick drive to the outdoor market. Tents have sprouted in orderly lines in a large parking lot, and hundreds of people mill about with cloth bags and wicker baskets. It's remarkable how this style of shopping is so fringe today, when it was the main way to sell goods for most of my life. The tents are uniform in size and style, the tables are plastic instead of wood, and the shoppers wear baseball caps and the women wear trousers, but if I half-close my eyes, I can pretend that I am elsewhere, elsewhen.

I park the car and we stroll toward the tents with Minnie's arm tucked in mine and her side comfortably pressing against me.

"What kind of fruit are you looking for?" I ask.

"Anything that looks delicious," she says. "Oh, look, honey. I should get some of that on the way back." We jostle through the crowd for a few more steps, then Minnie points. "Is that tent selling mushrooms? That's unusual. Let's have a look."

Mushrooms are hardly unusual to my mind, but I humor Minnie as she pulls me to the tent. Large piles of fungi sit in bins along the front of the table. The oyster mushrooms are a velvety gray, the shitakes a woodsy brown, and there are even some chanterelles of a mustard-yellow. Minnie points at a chanterelle.

"Do you like these? I have a recipe I'd like to try that calls for chanterelles." Her brow knits. "You know, I had one of my strange dreams last night, and where we are now reminds me exactly of the dream. You and I were in a market buying chanterelles—they were paler than these ones—and you wanted as many as we could fit in my basket. I was wearing a long red dress." She shakes her head. "Wow, déjà vu. Except for the red dress."

13

I stare at Minnie. I remember the scene she describes. It was in Venice, with my twelfth wife Zanetta. She was young, and we were still courting. Her stepmother was more discerning than her father—she saw through me, somehow, whereas her father was eager to marry his middle daughter to the well-spoken young noble from Rome.

"How strange," I say at last. "You're still having the dreams?"

"Yes. They don't bother me as much anymore. Perhaps I know you better now, so when you appear in my dreams, it's not as startling."

Minnie squeezes my arm and gives me a smile which I try to return, although my mind is bewildered. I still don't know why she is seeing my memories. So far, it is only memories of pleasant events with my lovers and wives. What if she starts dreaming of the battles I've fought or some of the more questionable periods of my life? I don't want to disturb her sleep with visions like that or have her see me in a different light.

"Do you want some ice cream?" Minnie points to a popular tent ahead, where two servers scoop colorful ice cream into waiting cones. "They make it locally."

I'm happy for the distraction, and we join the line. While Minnie speaks of a new mountaineering club she's thinking of joining, I examine her lauvan. Jen told me to be careful with Minnie. I want to find signs that she will weather a short-term relationship, that a fling will satisfy her, and she will not seek more from me. Her words and actions so far worry me, but the lauvan never lie.

Her navy-blue strands dance lightly with her happiness this morning. All well and good, but what of her feelings toward me? The lauvan that connect us are tightly woven together, but there are signs of fraying if I look closely. That is a good sign

14

for my purposes. I breathe a sigh of relief and smile at Minnie.

The hairs on my neck prickle. My eyes dart around to see what caused my reaction. After a moment's search, I find it: a tent of royal purple with two chairs and a small table underneath. A woman sits behind the table, which is draped with colorful scarves and spread with tarot cards. Her lauvan spasm with excitement. But it is not the fortuneteller who looks my way.

Anna Green stands beside the woman. Her eyes are fixed on mine, and when I meet her gaze, she gives me a small wave. Her eyes dart to Minnie with interest, and a spasm of some unidentifiable emotion crosses her face. She bends to speak with the fortuneteller then walks quickly through the crowd and disappears.

What was that about? It wouldn't surprise me if the fortuneteller was a Potestas member, which might explain Anna's visit to her tent. I couldn't read Anna's reaction at seeing Minnie by my side, and it worries me. It shouldn't—what would Anna do, and why?—but I can't shake a feeling of unease.

And what was the fortuneteller so excited by? Is Potestas up to something? My mind flits to the grail, buried deep underground. Surely no one could have found it. It's still there. Everything is fine.

But it can't hurt to check.

I'm distracted after my sighting of Anna, and although I try to hide it, Minnie is very perceptive.

"It looks like you have things to do," she says on the way to the car. "Why don't you drop me off and go do them?"

"No, I—"

"It's fine, Merry." She smiles and her strands wave to emphasize her words. "Call me later and we'll get together soon."

"I'd like that."

At Minnie's street, the only parking is a block away.

"I'll walk you to your door," I say. I pick up Minnie's bag of produce and get out of the car. Minnie joins me on the sidewalk, and I offer her my arm.

"How gallant." She smiles and links her arm through mine. We walk in companionable silence to her apartment building. Her arm is warm and soft and feels just right pressed against my side.

At the door, Minnie turns to face me. We are close now, very close. She gazes at me with a hint of a smile tugging at her lips.

"Thanks for walking me here, Merry." She looks at my mouth, then her eyes close and she leans forward to kiss me. I need no further encouragement. I let her cloth bag slither to the ground through my fingers and run my hands around her waist. Her lips are so soft and taste faintly of blackberry from the ice cream. Our lauvan twine together and I am brought to the giddiness of connection that overwhelmed me when we first danced. Every thought flies out of my mind, and all I want is to taste her delicious blackberry kiss.

I press her against the wall. Stucco scratches my fingers, but I don't care. Minnie's hands travel across my back, grip my hair, and it's all I can do not to groan at the sensation. Her lips open for me, and I almost bruise them with my hungry mouth. Our hips press into each other, but we're not close enough. I curse the layers of clothes that separate our bodies.

Minnie's hands leave my hair and press against my chest. I don't react to the pressure until she pushes more firmly, and

16

then my lips part from hers reluctantly.

"What's the matter?" I say hoarsely.

"Firstly, we're at my front door, with street traffic driving by and gawking." Her eyes dance. "Secondly, you have things to do."

"They can wait." I move to kiss her once more, but she puts a finger on my lips to stop me.

"You're distracted by whatever you need to do."

"Do I look distracted to you?"

"I don't want to be your means of procrastination." She smiles to soften her words, and her eyes laugh. "Come back when you are fully mine. I'll be waiting."

I growl in frustration, and she chuckles.

"Date on Wednesday? My evenings are full until then."

"You're going to make me wait three days to see you again?" I bow my head in defeat. "Cruel, cruel woman."

Her hand strokes my cheek gently.

"I'm looking forward to it."

She pats my chest then slides sideways. Only when the door closes behind her do I move. I shake my head and walk to my car. Minnie isn't wrong—the grail niggles at my mind like an itch that can't be scratched. But Minnie's hold on me, my attraction to her, can't be denied. Wednesday can't come soon enough.

It's not long before my car pulls over on the side of the road nearest the former sinkhole. I get out and approach the spot with trepidation, even as I tell myself that my fears are unfounded. How could anyone know where I hid it?

Excavator tracks and a gaping hole greet my disbelieving eyes. Someone was here, digging with heavy machinery. There is no reason for the city to dig here, and it is public property, so no homeowner would touch it. The only culprit is Potestas.

My heart sinks to my stomach. All that conniving on the

ship, the dangers I faced in the water to steal that damn cup, and it was stolen right back from me. How did they know? I'm certain I wasn't followed, and they could never have guessed. No person could have figured it out.

My eyes close and my head tilts back when I realize the truth. The spirits. Of course. Why do I keep leaving them out of my calculations? They dropped me in the hole, they found out about my power to repel them, and they likely sensed the strands of the grail in their domain. If March is as tight with the renegade spirits as she appears to be, it's the most likely explanation.

I pull out my phone and call Alejandro. While the burden of retrieving the grail falls on my shoulders, where it should, it's so pleasant to have confidantes to keep in the loop. I never tire of having friends.

"Hola?"

"Alejandro, bad news. I hid the grail, and Potestas found it. They have the grail."

Silence followed by a low whistle greets my ears.

"Now what?"

"Now we find it. I'll check at headquarters right now. Can you pass the news on to Jen? We need to come up with a plan to retrieve it."

"I'm on it."

It's time to hunt for the grail. Again.

The cupcake shop, Sweet Thing, is open for business. I pull the car over and stop the engine. I've only entered Potestas headquarters after hours. What's the protocol for entry? Is Potestas only an evening venture? On the positive side, there should be fewer people in my way once I find out how to enter. There must be some secret password that I am not privy to.

I deliberate, then I wrap my fingers around my lauvan and get to work. A few tweaks here and there produce a decent uniform, and my satchel quickly transforms to a toolbox.

The shop inside is bustling with happy mouths filled with colorful frosting. Two women at the counter pull out cupcakes from the glass counters and ring through purchases. I hold up my toolbox to the nearest attendant.

"Here for the dishwasher repair. Sorry I'm late."

The woman looks confused but is quickly distracted by a customer. She waves me through, and I slip behind the counter. There's a woman overseeing a large mixer and a man stocking shelves, but neither give me more than a cursory glance. When the women at the front are distracted, I open the door marked "plumbing" and slip through.

As I expected, the common area is nearly empty. There is one man lying on the far couch, but his eyes are closed, and he snores gently. I let go of my lauvan and my uniform dissolves back into my usual clothing.

I'm glad it's empty. I don't know what March has been told about the grail. The spirits must have told her where to dig, but did they tell her who buried it? How can she suspect anyone other than me, since I dived to retrieve it with her? Am I persona non grata at headquarters now? I will pretend nothing has changed and see how March reacts. Perhaps she thinks that the underwater grail was a fake, and that the real grail was buried in the ground the whole time.

I have free rein of headquarters, but where do I look? I can't imagine the common room being used for storage of such a precious item. March's office and the amulet acquisition room are far more likely. I walk down the hall on stealthy feet to the acquisition room. I'll start there, in case March is in her office.

I don't want my search halted before I can begin.

The room is empty of people. I enter and quietly close the door behind me. The floor-to-ceiling shelves that line the walls are filled with items of every description, from crosses to prayer flags, singing bowls to scraps of cloth. Most are religious in nature, and all are covered in a thick layer of multicolored lauvan.

The strands make it difficult for me to see the object underneath, but I know how big the grail is. And unless Potestas has added lauvan to the grail, I should still be able to see portions of its enameled bowl. My eyes scan the shelves, but nothing matches my memory of the cup.

There are plenty of objects, but after five minutes of searching I am confident that none is the grail. I sigh and open the door. I didn't really expect it to be in here with the regular amulets, but I had to check.

March's office is the next most likely room. There is still no one in sight, so I tread down the hall and knock gently on the office door. When there is no response, I pull the door open and slip inside.

March's desk is neat to the point of sparseness. There are no pictures, no pen holders, no blotter, only a closed laptop centered on the gleaming wood desk. Four drawers yield nothing but pens and file folders. I flip through one at the front. It contains a list of names and emails, along with notes about each name. Is this a list of Potestas members? I search for names I know. My name is halfway down the list, penciled in between Marty Lindstrom and David Mao, with a note beside it.

Unknown powers. Can see auras? Strong, took on Drew's spirit connection and won. Watch him.

I don't know how I can use this information, yet, but it's too good to pass up. I take a photograph with my phone of each page, five in all, then slide the sheets into the file folder. The other files are far less interesting—electricity invoices and the like—and the only other furniture in the room is a glass side table between two armchairs before the desk. I stand from my perusal of the drawers, defeated. I suspected March wouldn't leave the grail at Potestas unprotected, but I hoped. I'll glance around the library before I go, but it won't be there. I'm certain now that March has squirreled the grail away in her safe, the safe whose only key rests on March's bracelet.

The door clicks open and Anna Green enters. She jumps at the sight of me, then she puts a hand to her chest.

"Merry. You startled me." Her eyes narrow in suspicion. "What are you doing in here?"

"I was looking for March, but she's not here." I shrug my shoulders. "Better luck next time. When does she usually turn up?"

"Most evenings." Anna's lauvan are still in tight coils from her suspicion as I walk out the door, but she pastes on a smile when she catches me looking. If she knows about my grail switch, she doesn't let on. "You could try tonight. I'll be here then, too, if you want some company."

"Thanks, Anna." I don't follow up on her offer, and her lauvan droop slightly. "See you later."

Her eyes follow my back all the way to the exit, but my mind is on more pressing matters. How can I get the key from March?

I drive home, dispirited by the lack of grail at Potestas. The next logical place to search is March's safe, but the barriers to my hunt are significant. How will I retrieve the key, when the only copy dangles from March's bracelet? I have time—March said the ceremony would be no sooner than a week—so I can figure out this conundrum tomorrow.

21

CHAPTER IV

Dreaming

Abelin closes the door gently behind him. The group around me shudders at the clicking sound in the tight space of the attic. I walk softly toward him in socked feet, careful to avoid chalk marks on the floor that signify where the floorboards squeak.

"Did you get it?" I whisper. Abelin nods.

"There was a blockade that I had to avoid, then a convoy of Nazi officials stopped traffic for ages. But the truck is parked two blocks away. It's as close as I can get it."

"Good. I'll take this lot transformed." I jab my thumb at the party of eight terrified-looking people behind me. "Then I'll turn them back once they're in the truck. I don't see why I can't go with you the whole way, though. We could keep them transformed until they reach Vichy, or beyond."

"And what if you died, or were captured? Who would release them then?" Abelin says in a tone that pleads for reason in an irrational situation. "And anyway, we need you to cover our tracks. You're so good at confusing officials."

I sigh.

"I suppose I am. Fine. But you'd better be damn careful. And I'm changing your looks, until we get to the truck. We don't want you recognized."

Abelin nods, then turns to the huddled group.

"I'm glad you're ready. We will leave in a few minutes. The trip will not be pleasant but keep in your mind the reward at the end. Better times will come to our beautiful Dijon, but until then, we must find you a safe home. You have been told of the—" He glances at me briefly. "Unorthodox methods we use to bring Jews to safety. Please don't be alarmed or cry out.

We must maintain our quiet, so we remain hidden. Maël here will transform each of you into mice and hide you in his pocket while we walk the two blocks to the truck."

There are stifled gasps from the women, wide-eyed stares from the men, and open-mouthed wonder from a little boy at the front. I give him a wink.

"We will drive over the border to Vichy," Abelin continues. "It will be many hours, lying in a hidden compartment in the truck in very close quarters. Once in Vichy, we have a safe house where you can rest before your next journey. Any questions before we begin?"

The little boy raises his hand, and Abelin nods gravely at him.

"Can I be a white mouse, please, sir?" he whispers.

His mother shushes him with a panicked look at us, as if we would deny them help because of the boy's impertinence. I sit on my haunches to bring my eyes level with the boy.

"White? With pink or black eyes?"

"Pink," he whispers inaudibly, but his mouth moves with the word. I smile and wink again.

"It shall be done." I stand and turn to Abelin. "I'll change you first. Show them how it's done."

Abelin submits to my lauvan-prodding, as he has many times before. A few moments later, a strapping young Aryan specimen stands before us, and everyone gasps. I beckon the boy and his mother forward.

"Let's begin."

Within minutes, seven brown mice and one tiny albino mouse wriggle in the specially reinforced pocket of my wool overcoat. It's threadbare in places—there isn't much new to be had at any price in Dijon these days—but it holds my passengers firmly. Abelin nods at me and we tread softly down the stairs. At the bottom, we tie on our shoes and open a hidden door into my clock repair shop. Time ticks on, regardless of who is in control, and the Nazis and the French alike need their clocks in working order. The French can't pay much, but I inflate the German bills enough to get by.

I was tempted to leave once the rumors of occupation started flying, but I had finally created a comfortable life here after many years of wandering. I had a store, an apartment, friends—I figured I could weather any storm.

But this is a fierce storm, and when my good friend Abelin asked me to help smuggle persecuted Jews and grounded Allied airmen out of Dijon, I couldn't refuse. I was in this mess too deep, and some of the persecuted were my friends and neighbors. Besides, my unique skills lend themselves to smuggling.

The summer is unseasonably cool, although my wool coat is too much. I start to sweat from heat and nerves. The back street where my shop resides is quiet, since no one leaves their home unless necessary. Gone are the days of children playing in the square, women gossiping in the alleys, market stalls of fresh cheeses. I hope those days return, but as the months turn to years, I despair of this city ever seeing the light of freedom again.

We walk briskly, our boots splashing in puddles left by the morning's rainstorm. Around the corner, past Madame Rousselle's bakery, a shiny gray car zooms past. It sprays a sheet of water at us, and we jump out of its reach just in time. Abelin glances darkly at me, his ruddy-cheeked face looking odd with the expression. He jerks his blond head down the street toward the truck.

We're so close. Despite our best efforts at nonchalance, our footsteps speed up. There is a startled squeak from my pocket.

"Halt!"

A commanding voice stops us cold. It is a voice used to

authority. We turn to face our new obstacle.

A bespectacled man stands before us. He wears a tightly belted uniform with an officer's formed hat and a grim expression in his dark eyes. I place a warning hand over my pocketful of mice, and they grow still.

"Can we help you?" I say in accented German. Most of my countrymen have picked up only a few broken phrases of German, and my grasp of the language always seems to provide relief to the Germans. Whatever advantage I can glean, I do.

"Show me your papers," he says with a grunt. We wordlessly extract identification out of our pockets. Abelin hands his over nervously, but I wrap my fingers around the man's sand-colored lauvan and send my intentions his way. His eyes glaze, and he nods placidly.

"Good day," he says. Without a further word, he turns and marches down the empty street.

Abelin sags beside me with relief. A tiny patch of unpleasant wetness spreads to my trousers from my pocket—one of my passengers must have been too terrified for control. I nudge Abelin and we take great strides to the truck.

The back is empty, for the moment. Abelin will pick up cargo at our friend Germain's shop, a few minutes' drive away. I climb carefully into the back for the sake of the mice, and Abelin helps me open the secret compartment under the floor.

It's a tiny space, ridiculously small for the number of people we hope to cram in there, but this is not our first trip and I know they will fit. Every single one of them value their freedom over their comfort today.

One by one, I gently lift each mouse out of my pocket and unpick the lauvan knots. The tiny albino mouse I save for last, and the little boy lies on top of his mother once transformed.

"Good luck," I whisper to them all, and give the boy a wink.

Then Abelin and I place the false floor on top and spread burlap sacking for cover.

Outside, I embrace Abelin.

"Don't take any more risks than you must," I say.

"Keep them off our scent," he replies. "Give me a few days."

"Don't keep us waiting."

He gives me a lopsided grin.

"I'll be back."

When I awake, I recall that Abelin never returned. He was caught and killed on his way back with the empty truck. I continued my efforts in his memory, but when the war ended, I fled my prison of grief to find a new life in Central America. The wheel spins again and again, and the cycle of my life repeats.

CHAPTER V

My morning class passes without incident, and Wayne's knock on my office door is a welcome break from marking assignments. I push my rolling chair back.

"Hungry?" Wayne pokes his head through the doorway.

"Yes. This last paper was giving me a headache, it's so poorly written. I need a break."

"I hear you. I hate plowing through half-assed attempts," says Wayne with a roll of his eyes. "It takes forever."

"Oh, I don't bother reading them." I sling my satchel over my shoulder. "It's an immediate re-write. I have the time to read it, but certainly not the inclination. No, it's the sheer fact that someone bothered to print out such rubbish that makes my head pound."

Wayne laughs and follows me to the rooftop door.

"I like that strategy. I might implement it on the really terrible papers."

Wayne unlocks the door with a quick glance around to make sure nobody watches us—we're not supposed to have the key to the roof—and I trail up the stairs after him. The roof is sunny but with a biting breeze that reminds me of autumn, despite it being mid-summer. The seasons pass me by like leaves in the wind.

Wayne bites into a deli sandwich while I dig out a bun and hunk of cheese from my satchel. It's all that I felt like wrangling together from my fridge this morning, although it's not so different from thousands of midday meals I've consumed over the centuries. The bread is much whiter, though.

"Coming to lunch club at the gym this week?" Wayne asks through a mouthful of sandwich. Wayne gave me a standing invitation to join his mixed martial arts fight club once a week. I've gone a few times, and it's a great way to remind my body how to move again, after many years of peaceful disuse. Who knows when I might need my skills sharp once more? And I can't deny that I enjoy a good fight. This way, I can make friends and punch them at the same time. Who could ask for more?

"Wouldn't miss it."

"What's the status on Potestas?" Wayne licks mustard off his thumb then swats away a curious wasp. "I heard about the stolen grail. How do we stop this ceremony from happening, now that March has it?"

"I believe they have almost everything they need to proceed. And once they complete the ceremony, spirits will possess the members of Potestas, and I don't know what will happen then." My skin crawls at the thought of spirit possession, of not being in control of my own body. "These people have no idea what they're getting into. The spirits have an agenda they're not sharing with the organization, I'm certain of it. The best way to stop this is to take away the grail, which is easier said than done."

"Do you know where it is?"

"I looked at headquarters but came up empty-handed. March must have it at her house, so I'll have to dig deeper. If that doesn't work, I might need backup. Are you in?"

Wayne nods decisively.

"Of course. Ready and waiting."

"Good. It might come to that." I sigh and toss a crust to a waiting crow. "I hate saving people from themselves. I'd much rather smack sense into them instead."

We watch two crows fight each other for the crust. The first crow yanks it away from the second and flies to a nearby tree. The other caws with raucous indignation.

28

"Have you felt the earthquakes lately?" Wayne asks after a pause. I shake my head.

"Should I have?"

"A friend of mine in the geology department mentioned that they've measured unusual earth tremors in the past few days. I haven't felt anything either—they're probably too deep for us surface-dwellers to sense. I wonder what's going on down there."

"What comforting news, when my apartment was built before plate tectonic theory was proposed." I raise an eyebrow at Wayne, who chuckles.

"You should always be ready for the big one, Merry. You never know when it will come."

I have few classes in the summer, so by midafternoon I throw my satchel on my coffee table at home and flop onto the couch. There are a few moments of silence, silence so thick and still that traffic noise from outside sounds distant and tinny. It's very quiet without Alejandro, and even quieter knowing that he won't bang through the door at any moment.

I release a deep sigh then lean forward and slide my old friend Braulio's notebook toward me from its current place on the coffee table. My fingers idly flip through the pages. I've read it all before, but perhaps there is more to learn. What I'd really like to do is peruse Potestas' library, but I'll be stopped if I don't have a disguise. March doesn't trust me enough to allow me free rein of her books.

The notebook, filled with findings that Braulio compiled over a lifetime of research into the spirit world, is organized by element. Fire is first, its pages illuminated by diagrams of orange flames and crucibles. The air section has stylized diagrams of a puffing north wind and misty apparitions. I'm impressed by Braulio's artistic talents and saddened that I can't tell him so anymore. It was only a few short months ago that he died, and the memory still smarts.

The water pages contain illustrations of still lakes and bubbling pots, along with copious notes on naiads and sirens, mermaids and whirlpools, and the spells of protection that served me well when water spirits were aggressively attempting to communicate with me. I flip to the next section.

I haven't delved into the earth section with as much intensity as the other three, so I slowly flip the pages. Fragments of sentences enter my mind as I casually skim the text. Pictures of sacred mountains and altars in dripping caves abound. My stomach tightens at an illustration of a cleft in the earth, looking remarkably like the sinkhole I fell into the other day. Those spirits who contacted me were earth spirits, but I don't feel the need to fight them. I'd rather hear what they have to say. They tease me with knowledge of my father and leave me wanting more, needing more.

I don't feel helpless against them, not the way I did against the water spirits from before. I managed to scare the earth spirit in that sinkhole, which felt good. I feel on firmer footing now. Perhaps it is because they aren't the first spirits I've tackled, and my experience is helping. Whatever the reason, I'm more confident in my dealings.

That doesn't mean it isn't smart to have a few tricks up my sleeve. I bend over the notebook to learn more and start reading at random.

These philosophers debated the nature of the animus behind each tree, each mountain, each earthquake. Were they immortal or not? And if not, did they reproduce as do the animals of Earth, or perhaps are reborn as is the phoenix from the flame?

From the rigid class system of their birth, the philosophers naturally examined the nature of classes of spirit and attempted to categorize them based on power. The smallest, weakest spirits were connected to the ephemeral flowers of the meadows and grains of sand on the beaches. Larger phenomena, such as mountains or destructive events like earthquakes or landslides, were credited to the ruling spirits. These, of course, are the most frequently worshiped in many cultures, a fact which was not lost upon our intrepid philosophers.

I wonder how much truth lies in the rambling thought experiments of centuries ago. It's irrelevant to my current goal of learning methods of defense, so I flip to the next page.

After a few minutes of reading, I look at my watch. I have a chess game to win at Gary's apartment next door, and he's expecting me now. My reading will have to wait.

Gary opens the door at my knock. His wrinkled face beams at me and his lauvan wave.

"Merry, come in, come in. I've been reading about a few new tactics that I can't wait to try on you. I might even win this game."

"You can keep trying, Gary," I say with a smile. "But don't beat yourself up about it. An old guy like you…"

I leave the sentence dangling, and Gary laughs heartily. I've never known him to take offense to anything.

"Don't underestimate the elderly, my young friend. Experience counts for a lot."

"I suppose it does." And that's the reason I win. "I can't

have you winning easily. I'm here to keep your brain sharp."

"Sharp as a brass tack, all right." Gary chuckles and shuffles into the kitchen. I settle onto a dining room chair in front of the chess board, and he comes back with a plate of cookies.

"The missus baked these this morning before her bridge club."

"She's a good woman," I say.

"The very best."

We set up the chess board, and Gary chats about what he and his wife did yesterday, and how his grandkids are. I let him chatter. It's a welcome change from my silent apartment next door. When he pauses for a breath, I remember what Alejandro told me about Gary last week.

"Did you used to skydive, Gary? Alejandro mentioned it to me."

Gary's face lights up at my interest, and I understand the reaction Alejandro draws out of people, why they open up to him the way they do.

"Yessir, I was an instructor for years. Oh, there's nothing like leaping into thin air, nothing but a hope of a parachute on your back, the world almost too far away to see. It's something else. Did you ever try?"

"Once, years ago." It was exhilarating, but I can achieve a more controlled effect as a falcon. "It was incredible, but not something I wished to repeat."

"I met plenty like you on the job," Gary says with a faraway gleam in his eye. "I could get them to come back at least half the time. There was this one fellow…"

While Gary recalls his storied past, I nod in the right places and observe his lauvan. The threads are still close to his body, unlike mine. He sloughs off strands frequently, as is common with the elderly, and he has many connections that splinter away from his body into transparency in different directions. Compared to my loose cloud, his lauvan are tightly coiled. What's the difference between us? I have centuries on him, certainly, but why don't his strands appear looser than my younger friends? I grow weary of mysteries that can never be solved, and tune into the conversation once more.

"Time for a game?" Gary rubs his hands together. "You'll see, youngster, I have a few tricks up my sleeve today."

"I'll believe it when I see it." I grin at him and he chuckles.

"Let's get this show on the road."

Gary tends to favor his knights while playing, but my piece of choice is the bishop—always sliding in at an unpredictable angle and catching other players off guard. No doubt, Gary has some slick moves from long practice, but to me they are easy to predict. Sometimes, I let him get close to checking my king, but never allow my defeat entirely. His strands clearly show his thrill at almost beating me, and he never dissolves into disappointment. He adores the challenge.

"Do you have big plans for tonight, young man?" Gary says after capturing my rook.

"Quiet night in, I expect. Alejandro moved out, so quieter than usual."

"A good kid, that one. Hold onto your friends, Merry. They make life worth living, have your back when you're down." He slaps my shoulder with a guffaw. "Give you someone to drink with."

I grin.

"No doubt."

"I'm just saying, don't let your new friendship with Alejandro fade just because he's living in a different apartment. Good people don't come into your life every day, after all. Why do you think I put up with the missus?" He laughs. "She's good people, and worth the occasional nagging into my deaf ear."

"You're right," I say, and move my bishop. "I'll call Alejandro tomorrow. Checkmate."

"What?" Gary peers at the board then nods in approval. "Dang it, you're right. After I got your queen, I thought for sure I had it in the bag. Good game, Merry."

CHAPTER VI

Dreaming

I sink onto the dry dirt before a crackling campfire and sigh with contentment. It has been a pleasantly dry stretch of summer lately, and it is comfortable to be able to lounge by the fire without damp boots and a damper cloak. Sounds of the men preparing food drift through the night air, and the forest is dotted with fires surrounded by glowing faces. Gareth hands me a stick skewered with charred chunks of meat.

"Dinner for you, Merlin," he says with an amiable smile. "I hope you enjoy it. Game was hard to come by this afternoon, but a rat valiantly gave his life to be your supper."

I take the stick and tear off some meat with my teeth then chew thoughtfully until I swallow. Arthur looks nauseated beside Gawaine as he holds a half-eaten skewer of meat.

"Nice try, Gareth. But I've eaten enough rat to know it when I taste it." I grin at him. "Rat's not bad, only too chewy for my liking. I much prefer rabbit." I hold up the stick in salute.

Gareth throws back his close-cropped blond head with a guffaw that splits his broad face in a wide smile.

"The joke was too good to pass up. I didn't expect you to be a rat-eater."

"I'll take that as a compliment."

"But it's truly rabbit?" Arthur says with an attempt at joviality, although he eyes his meat with distrust. I point my skewer at him.

"There's your joke's payoff, Gareth. Go on, Arthur, meat is meat. It wouldn't hurt your soft lord's stomach to experience a little rat."

"Soft, am I?" Arthur's eyes flash with amused indignation.

"I'll remember that the next time you need saving from a sword in your side."

"Are you still harping on about that? Yes, I am eternally grateful that you watch my back in battle." I take another bite and speak through my mouthful. "But keep bringing it up and I'll have to remind you of all the battles that I've watched yours."

"And you two would be nowhere without me," Gawaine adds with a smug pat on his massive chest.

"If we're all finished measuring our swords," says Gareth. "Mine's the largest, by the way—can anyone tell me when we're expecting to arrive at the villa?"

"Can't wait to reintroduce your sword to your wife, I suppose," I say. Gawaine snorts, but Arthur answers Gareth's question.

"If we push hard, we should be there by sunset. I'm sure your children will be happy to see you also." He smiles at Gareth, whose eyes light up at the thought, but there is an air of sadness around Arthur that likely only I can see. He and Guinevere have been married for years, and never once has Guinevere shown signs of being with child. Arthur rarely speaks of it, but I know it pains him. They have asked me to examine their lauvan for problems, but I cannot find anything clearly wrong. Sometimes nothing can be done, even by me. I try to lighten his mood with a jest.

"It's a good thing the little runts are yours and not mine," I say. Gareth's twins are hardly runts, and instead take after their father in size. "I can't imagine being tied down with a pair of ankle-nibblers."

Gareth chuckles, taking no offense to my ribbing. He's the most good-natured man I've ever met.

"Nor tied down to one woman, it would seem."

"There's something to be said for having a good woman

waiting for you at the end of a long campaign," Gawaine adds. His own wife is a recent development, but Gawaine has wasted no time in giving her a round belly to match her apple cheeks.

"You'll find her one day," Gareth says, strangely solemn. "She'll make you, Merlin."

I wave him off.

"One woman? Forever? I'll believe it when I meet her. Until then…" I grin.

There is a scuffling and shouts from the edge of our encampment. We all tense, but whatever occurred appears to be subdued. Moments later, Arthur's eyes narrow as two sentries approach our fire, a stranger clutched between them.

"My lord Arthur," says one of our men. "We were on sentry duty and caught this intruder. Might be a spy." He shakes the central man's arm for emphasis. The man cringes, his eyes fearful under a mop of dark hair. He glances at each of us in turn, but his gaze stops at my face. He jerks as if scalded and would back away if the guards didn't have a firm grip on his arms. I glance at Arthur, who looks as confused as me at the man's reaction.

"Do you know me?" I ask him. He avoids my gaze.

"I know of you, lord Merlin. The stories say—" He gulps.

"Tell me more." I lean back on my hands. "I do love a good story. How does my reputation precede me?"

"Your sorcery is well-known," he mumbles to his boots. His knees are actually trembling. I feel Gareth, Arthur, and Gawaine glance at each other. They all know of my abilities, but for the sake of the guards, I feign ignorance.

"I wish I did have sorcery, because I could force you to tell us who you were spying for, and why. Then I could change you into a frog." Arthur turns his face away to hide his smile. I've done that very thing to him in the past. "But since it isn't true, I'll let you tell your story to lord Arthur. But, don't forget, there are ways other than sorcery to make you talk."

The man grows even more pale but turns when Arthur speaks.

"Who do you work for? You don't look Saxon."

"I won't tell you anything," he squeaks out. He glances at me again. I grin and flex my fingers threateningly. Gareth smothers his laugh in a cough.

"All right!" the man blurts out. "The Lady Morgan sent me. She needs to know where you are, so you don't thwart her plans."

"Which are?" Arthur says with a patient air.

"She means to attack the Saxon settlement at the border of Caer-Magnis."

"They're part of the truce," Arthur says with frustration. "How many times must I fix Morgan's mistakes?"

"You should have seized her lands when her husband Idris died, years ago," I say.

"I made the right decision at the time, but now I wonder." Arthur sighs then signals the guards to take the spy away. "Shackle him. We'll take him with us. And alert the men that we're going to Caer-Magnis first."

The guards depart. Gareth's shoulders slump.

"So close," he murmurs.

CHAPTER VII

I've been pacing around the room, listening to the discussion of my students. Some conversations have been blisteringly dull, others shine with concealed insight, like uncut diamonds. At the front, I wait for them to quiet down. It takes only a few seconds—they all have half an eye on me, waiting for my direction. Having command of a room is a handy skill.

"What have you discussed?" I ask the hushed room. "How does the poem *Beowulf* treat Grendel's mother? Michael."

They hate it when I choose someone instead of letting the most forward volunteer. That's part of the fun. They stay on their toes this way. Michael looks resigned as he opens his mouth.

"She's one of the three monsters that Beowulf has to defeat. The poem describes her as a hag who dragged the hero down to her creepy cave, where he has to fight her to win."

"Yes, that's how she is described in the text. I'm looking for interpretation of how the poem portrays her. Kristal?"

A young woman on the side crinkles her nose in irritation at being called, but she gamely offers her thoughts.

"Well, she's clearly a murdering monster, but the only reason she did it was in revenge. Beowulf did just kill her son. The poem doesn't really empathize, though. It's all about Beowulf and the battles."

"Indeed. It pays to look at the villain's motivations. Even if their actions don't justify their means, deeper understanding can be obtained from that analysis. All right, that's enough for today." The class begins to scrape back chairs and pull out backpacks, but I raise my hand, and everyone stills. "I recommend you jot down the gist of your discussions. They will come in useful for your next paper."

I drop my hand and the class resumes its noisy departure. Once the first few students barge out of the door, another figure slips inside. My frown of confusion changes to one of annoyance. What is Anna Green doing at my place of work? She sees me at the Potestas headquarters often enough, and she knows where I live. She doesn't need to seek me out here.

Anna is dressed in skin-tight jeans and an alluring blouse that pretends to be demure while it clings to her curves. She has paired the outfit with heels and a knowing smile, and sashays to the front of the class. The eyes of my students follow her with curiosity.

"Merry," Anna says when she reaches me. "How are you?"

I give her a hard look.

"Why are you here, Anna?"

She pouts.

"You'll give me a complex. I'm not that repulsive, am I?" She gives the nearby Michael a sideways glance and smiles. He ducks his head and scurries past, embarrassed to be caught looking. I sigh.

"Spit it out."

"Fine," she says, but without real rancor. "I was told to bring you this."

She pulls out a wristband of leather that she had somehow squeezed into her jeans' pocket. It is embedded with a deep maroon garnet, and it is thick with lauvan, all earth ones. Their brown strands intertwine slowly, some silvery brown, some the black of freshly-turned loam, some the living brown of a tree trunk.

Anna holds it out to me, but I don't take it immediately.

"Who told you? Why are you giving me—" I look around the room, but all my students have left. "An amulet? Will it do something to me?"

"So suspicious. Nothing will happen to you, I promise."

Anna shakes the wristband in my direction with impatience, and I gingerly take it between two fingers. The earth lauvan meet my own questing strands, but do not engage in any worrying way.

"See? It's fine," she says. "We were given instructions to give you a way to contact the spirit world. Apparently, you're special." She winks at me. "But I knew that already. I don't know how it will work, but they said you would figure it out."

"Who are they?" Is there someone else behind Potestas, more than March?

"The spirits, of course." Anna looks puzzled at my confusion. "They didn't give us many details. Do you know why they want to talk? I'm dying to know."

I shake my head slowly, but it's a lie. I'm this son they search for. And now, maybe, I have a chance to find out more answers, contact the spirits on my terms. Will they be more forthcoming now that they have provided me this line of communication? Will I find out who this "successor" is?

"Sorry, I'm stumped." I hold out the wristband for a better look. "I suppose it has a sort of rustic charm. Do you think it's my style?"

Anna sighs with exasperation.

"Your talents are wasted on you. Honestly, Merry. I can't wait to join with my spirit. Then I'll show you how to live." She backs away, shaking her head. "Good luck, Merry. I hope you know more than you let on."

Anna turns and saunters away. I watch her curvy backside exit the room as a matter of course, but as soon as she leaves my attention is fully on the wristband. Am I ready to talk to the spirits?

I am ready.

I stare at the wristband. How can I contact the spirits?

Certainly not in this classroom, where any curious student can spy on me muttering, seemingly to myself. My office is little better, as the walls are paper thin, and I don't wish to alert my colleagues to my strange behavior.

It must be now, though. I can't wait another moment. This is my chance to take control of my dealings with the spirits, these mysterious beings who promise so many answers to questions I've asked for centuries. Over and over in the past few weeks I've come tantalizingly close to answers, but always at the spirits' behest. I want the control for once.

I have no more classes today, so I shove the wristband into my pocket and head for the door. I need somewhere quiet and private. I have a sense that outdoors will help—Anna contacted her fire spirits for the volcano at Wallerton in a park—so I jog away from campus into the nearby woodland.

It's a breezy day, but I'm still sweating lightly after ten minutes along woodchip-lined trails. The space beneath the coniferous trees is dim and cool, and I pass only two other joggers. They eye me with bemusement as I run past in slacks and buttoned shirt.

At a thick patch of Oregon grape bush, I leave the path. There is enough cover that I can hide behind a cluster of trees and not be seen. Once ensconced between three close firs and a patch of shoulder-height ferns, I pull out the wristband and twist it slowly in my hands.

Now what? How do I go about contacting the spirits? And, most importantly, how do I do so while keeping control over myself?

Anna said I would know what to do. The spirits know of my abilities with the lauvan, but what do they think I know?

I let my lauvan prod and poke the serenely swirling earth lauvan. The chocolate brown of my strands blends in with the many different earth tones that surround the wristband.

The earth lauvan respond. They wrap around mine gently but firmly, and I feel pressure on my fingertips. I grip the wristband more securely and watch in fascination as the earth strands multiply. They bloom from their perch on the leather to cover my hands, my arms, my torso, entwining with my own. I am still and tense, barely breathing. What is happening? Can I escape if I need to? Do I want to?

As suddenly as they boiled forth, they retreat to the wristband and leave me with a lingering tingle on my skin. But instead of calming down to swirl once more around the leather, they twist up in a mass level with my head. Two long bulges extend on either side, and a gap forms near the top, above where the lauvan narrow. I am forcibly reminded of the spirit forms that visited Anna back in Wallerton, the ones that were shaped like crude approximations of humans. The gap—mouth—opens wider.

"Greetings, son of earth." The spirit-shape's voice is gravely and deep. My eyes widen with shock, although I keep the wristband held out with steady hands to support the spirit.

"Greetings," I reply hoarsely. What does it mean, calling me a "son of earth?" That I'm human, I suppose. That must be how the spirits refer to us. I clear my throat. "Thank you for coming. I have so many questions."

"Indeed." The spirit doesn't say more. The silence stretches for a moment, while earth strands tickle my own.

"Yes, right." My mind whirls with questions. What do I ask first? "Why did you tell Anna to give me the amulet? Why did you want me to contact you? Who is the person you work for, this successor of my father? What do you know about my father?"

The spirit waits until I pause for breath.

"You have many questions, son of earth. You know little of your heritage, must less than we supposed. These answers are

43

best supplied by the successor. But our comrade is not able to speak with you now. Once the ritual is complete, and we walk among you, the successor will tell you all."

My jaw clenches. How long must I wait? I don't want to sit down for a cozy chat with this "successor." I want answers.

"Give me the basics. We can hash out the details later."

The mouth gap widens in a smile.

"All in good time. The successor wished for a simpler way of contacting you that did not involve rending the earth, hence, this amulet. You are stronger than we supposed, and that interests the successor. But first, we must ask you this: where do your loyalties lie?"

I frown. What does loyalty mean to a spirit? Is there a battle that I'm unaware of? My first thought is loyalty to the long-dead Arthur, or to my beautiful wives, but I doubt either of those answers would make sense to the spirits.

"I suppose I'm loyal to myself. There is only ever me, in the long-run."

The mass of lauvan that acts as the spirit's head nods briskly, as if it approves of that answer.

"And do you know why you can see the elements?" the spirit asks in its hoarse voice. "You can see my current form, for example. That is a rare ability."

"No," I breathe. "No, I have never known how I can."

"We can tell you," the spirit states simply. "But we want your help first. The ritual must take place. Help us come to Earth, and we will tell you everything."

There it is, the answers I've searched for my whole life, dangling like a fruit on a tree, just out of reach. It would be so easy to let the ritual happen. All I have to do is to stop trying to thwart March, and she will carry on with her preparations. The ritual could happen within days, and I wouldn't have to lift a finger. And then—then, I might solve the greatest

44

mystery of my life. And who knows what possibilities will be in my grasp then? What powers might I have? Could I find out where human lauvan go when the body dies? Could I change a lover's threads, so they could stay with me forevermore?

But what would I unleash in the process? What do the spirits plan, once they have human bodies to control? And what of those bodies, stolen from the people who once owned them? How many lives are my answers worth?

I am silent with indecision, but the spirit is satisfied that I haven't said no.

"We will speak again soon. Let the ritual take place, and everything will become clear, son of earth. We look forward to it."

Within seconds, the earth lauvan collapse into themselves, then swirl peacefully around the wristband. I stare at the leather for a moment, then sigh and put it back into my pocket. Again, I have nothing but questions. And now, I must decide what I value more: answers, or innocent lives.

I walk slowly back to my office, lost in thought. My classes are finished for today, and I have a meeting to attend at Potestas tonight. My satchel collected, I meander to my car. A student says hello in passing, but the greeting barely registers. I only come to myself when I turn the key in my car's ignition and the engine roars to life.

Right. The Potestas meeting tonight. I need to be on my toes. The invitation—which arrived in my inbox yesterday—was sparse on details but assured me that I didn't want to miss this gathering. Surely, it's too soon for the ceremony to bring the spirits to Earth? Either way, I need to be there, to find out what is happening, and to stop events if they get out of hand.

Assuming I want to stop the ritual. My stomach twists with the thought of the answers promised me. I stamp on the accelerator in frustration and pass a dawdling minivan ahead.

The cupcake shop is closed at this time, and I slip inside the unlocked entrance and through the secret door to Potestas' headquarters. A barrage of sound assaults my ears when I enter. The entire membership of the organization must be here tonight. Every couch and chair is occupied, it's standing-room only in the kitchen, and throngs line the hallways. The anticipation in the air is palpable, and they all chat eagerly to their neighbors.

I hear my name from nearby and rake my eyes across the crowd until I spot Esme, a slight acquaintance from a few days prior. I took her form when Alejandro and I snuck into headquarters to search the library. I hope she never finds that out.

Esme's fleshy cheeks quiver with excitement below her dyed black locks. Her fire-engine red mouth opens to greet me.

"Merry, dear, so glad you could make it."

"Hello, Esme. It's busy tonight."

"Yes, everyone is so thrilled that the ritual will take place soon. And all thanks to you! I hear your diving expedition went swimmingly." She nudges my side and I give her the grin she expects for her double-entendre.

"It did. Now we have the grail. Is there any impediment to holding the ceremony right now?"

I'm certainly not advocating rushing things, but I need to know what else must happen. How long do I have to stop events from unfolding? How long do I have to decide what I want?

Esme's brow wrinkles in thought.

46

"I think there's one more thing, but I can't recall. March should let us know tonight."

I nod, but before I can say any more, the doors to the central meeting room open wide. March and Anna stand against either door and greet people as they file inside. I am reminded of a priest greeting his flock, and I wonder at the power March wields with these people. They love her and are willing to follow her questionable decisions. How far can she push them?

I follow Esme to the entrance. While she enthusiastically greets March as she passes, I try to tread in the middle to avoid contact with either Anna or March. Anna gives me a glance and a nod, which I return. March, however, gazes at me after Esme enters the room. Her look is curious, searching. There's a hint of a confused smile, as if she knows something I don't, but isn't certain about it. She gives no indication that she suspects my hand in the burying of the grail. I nod, and she slowly gives one in return before her attention is diverted to the next member.

I take a seat near the back and wait until all are seated. Anna slips past once the room is full and takes a seat near the front. March closes the doors with a soft thump, and the chattering crowd grows still. She paces down the corridor with measured steps, confident in the silence. At the front, she turns to face us with a smile and open arms.

"Welcome, my friends. And thank you for coming here tonight, to this very special meeting. This is an exciting time to be a member of Potestas. We are so close to achieving our goals." She raises her hand and holds her thumb and forefinger a hair's breadth apart. "This close. Can you feel it?"

A murmur of agreement ripples through the audience. The faces that surround me are rapt, their eyes fixed on March. She continues her speech.

"But tonight, we must decide something very important.

47

The first ritual will allow three of our members to unite with their spirit traveler." Noises of consternation float in the air. March raises her hand. "Don't worry, everyone will have their turn. This is what we've worked so hard for, after all. Tonight, we must choose the lucky three who will be first. I would like those who wish to be the ground-breaking pioneers, to carve a path into the future for the rest of us, to come forward. Anna will take your names, and then we will do a draw."

March steps back to indicate that she is finished speaking. Clothes rustle and feet thud as nearly a third of the crowd files into the aisle. The volunteers glow with anticipation. Those who are still seated vary in their expressions. Some look curious, some uneasy, and some whisper to their neighbors with looks of fearful longing.

Anna stands at the front with a pen and a stack of index cards. On each one she writes a name as the hopefuls come forward, then drops it into a large glass bowl that sits on the marble pedestal. March stands to one side and gazes at her flock with an inscrutable look. Once all have given their names and been seated once more, Anna places the last card in the bowl and takes her seat. Neither she nor March wrote her own name on a card for the bowl, and I wonder why. March is a smart woman, as evidenced by her business acumen and her handling of this organization. She must have calculated the risks involved with this spirit possession and decided she was willing to wait for her powers, if it meant others could test the process first. No one is as successful as her without a certain level of caution and an eye for evaluating risk. She must be fond enough of Anna to tell her to wait as well, although Anna doesn't look happy about it. She vacillates between throwing March disgruntled looks and staring longingly at the bowl of names.

March steps forward, and the hushed room becomes

completely silent. The man beside me might even be holding his breath.

"Three volunteers will be chosen tonight. Three fortunate souls will gain the power of their dreams in the upcoming ritual. Three members of our organization will be the first to usher in the new era." March lifts her hand to the bowl. "Without further ado, I will select the names. After the meeting, please come forward and I will instruct you in the preparations you need for the ritual."

March plunges her hand into the bowl of names and selects an index card with strong fingers. She reads it swiftly, then looks up at the room.

"Thomas Ober."

"Yes!" A middle-aged man in the front leaps to his feet. The crowd claps and whistles. Those who did not put their names in clap with genuine enthusiasm. Those who did shift their eyes from Thomas to the bowl and sit on the edge of their seats, anxious for March to draw another name.

March reaches into the bowl before the applause finishes and extracts another name.

"Esme Rotari."

Esme jumps up with more vigor than I expected from someone of her age and stature. She throws her hands in the air and whoops. Those around her laugh and clap at her joy.

The applause is much shorter this time. The focus is on March's hand in the bowl. She fishes around for a moment, then pulls out one last card. The silence is absolute.

"Ben Hart."

Ben rises with a blissful look on his face as two-thirds of the crowd erupts with applause. The other third, those who were not selected, slowly put their hands together in sad imitations of clapping. Their doleful faces make me wonder what their stories are, what pushed them into joining Potestas with a promise of power to be gained. What are they escaping? What wrongs need to be put right in their lives?

March raises her hand for quiet. Ben sits and the audience hushes.

"Congratulations, Thomas, Esme, and Ben." She smiles at each with beneficence and they beam back at her. "You will truly be pioneers in our brave new world. But the rest of you, your time will come. I am as anxious as any to join with my spirit traveler, and we will continue to hold rituals until everyone who wishes it is connected. There is so much good we will do once we are all joined. Our combined powers will be great enough to meet the injustices of the world head-on. Potestas will be a beacon of light."

March pauses for a moment, and the crowd leans forward to hear her next words.

"There is one more thing we need for the ritual, one more thing we haven't collected. It's why I haven't yet set a date for the ritual. We are currently searching for a person with an exceptionally strong aura. Arnold and Anna have special amulets that allow them to sense someone with this requirement, and it's only a matter of time before one is revealed. Once we have found a suitable candidate, the ritual will take place. Unfortunately, the aura of this person will need to be stripped away to open the spirit world, which will cause the person to pass away."

Pass away? I stare at March in shock and revulsion. She's speaking of human sacrifice, couched in a palatable euphemism. It's been many centuries since I've been party to a human sacrifice, and I didn't care for it then. How can March justify this atrocity to herself? There are a few mutterings from the crowd, but most wait to hear what March has to say next, perhaps hoping that she will ease any guilt they might feel.

"However, only one person will be enough for many, many

rituals. It's regrettable, but this sacrifice is for a much greater cause. The powers we will have will allow us to change the world, for the better. One life will be taken, but so many lives will be saved."

For the greater good? I've heard that line many times in my life, and it's always a slippery slope. I don't deny that sometimes it's true, but the line between acceptable and not is very hard to see, and it's easy to justify any action with enough talk.

Most in the crowd seem outwardly mollified by March's words, although there are a few sideways glances between neighbors. March wraps up the meeting with words of parting and waves the three volunteers forward. The rest shuffle out of the room. I stay in my seat until the crowds disperse.

I have my answer, now. I can't allow this ritual to proceed. I could possibly stand aside while the members of Potestas willingly allow themselves to be possessed, but I draw a line in the sand at murdering an innocent. If I don't step in, no one else will, by the looks of it. It doesn't matter what answers the spirits have for me. I must stop them.

CHAPTER VIII

Dreaming

I stretch my aching back and think longingly of massaging the knots out of my lauvan tonight, when no one is looking. My host family in the village goes to bed early and leaves me time on my own before the banked fire. I might be young, but hard work affects me the same as any other.

"Pick up the pace, Merlin," my druid master Orin calls from behind me.

"A moment's rest, that's all I took," I mutter back, but I bend to pick up a bundle of branches for the bonfire.

"We have much to do before the ceremony," Orin says. "We must all do our share." He moves off to oversee another group of students toiling to fill a cart with wood. My friend Pert puffs up beside me.

"It's a lot of work," Pert says. "But think of what we might achieve. We could hear spirits tonight. For the first time in fourteen years!"

"Yes, if you are gullible." I shuffle the branches in my arms and trudge to the cart.

"You don't believe in the spirits?" Pert says.

"No. Why should I? I've never heard or seen anything like that." Surely if spirits were real, I would have seen something with the lauvan, but there has never been a sign. I nudge Pert with my shoulder. "I think those who claim to have heard spirits ate too much belladonna."

Pert laughs but sobers when Orin speaks behind us.

"You have a skeptic's mind, Merlin. It will keep you careful in life but take care not to let it override every situation. As for the spirits, they are indeed real. Where do you think those with the ability to sense storms, hear answers in the rain, and feel fire without burning came from? Those with special abilities are the descendants of spirits from long ago."

A quick retort dies on my lips as I ponder his words, but I dismiss my questions quickly. Orin is wise, but he can't see what I do.

"I'll haul wood for the fire, but I'll believe in spirits when I hear them."

Orin nods his head.

"I expect nothing else." He waves at the cart. "When this is full, please take a meal to the guards for the prisoner."

"Who's the prisoner?" Pert asks.

"A slave who disobeyed. We need a sacrifice for the ceremony tomorrow, so he will fulfill that role."

Orin walks away to shout at two students who wrestle with an oversized log. I turn to Pert.

"Did you know we were killing someone for this?"

Pert shrugs.

"No. But if it brings us closer to the spirits... And the slave would have been punished, in any event."

"Not with death." I gaze with consideration at Pert until he squirms.

"What do you want to do about it? The ceremony must go on—"

"Must it?"

"Yes, it must. This is our big chance to contact the spirit world once more! The moon is in the right phase, everything is prepared. And the masters think it is fine, so it must be all right."

I gaze at Pert with narrowed eyes. He had never struck me as a mindless sheep until now. My respect for him flickers. I've thought lately about whether the path to become a druid is the one I want to follow to completion. I wonder if today I have finally made up my mind. To follow orders blindly is not in my nature.

My stomach clenches at the thought of leaving. For two whole years I've had food, shelter, friends, purpose. Can I truly throw that all away? What will I do? Where will I go?

But I can't be party to murder in cold blood, especially for such a ridiculous goal. I am done here, but I can't let the others know. They will not take kindly to me deserting my studies, nor to what I plan to do before I go. I grin at Pert.

"You're right, of course. Come, perhaps we can sneak some cheese when we collect the guard's meals."

The village is silent under the full moon. I open the door of my host family's cottage with care and slip out of the gap. Behind me on the hearth lie three wooden dolls I fashioned out of wood using my knife and lauvan skills before I left. It's a poor thanks for the care and hospitality they have shown me, but their three little daughters will hopefully enjoy the presents.

I walk noiselessly past silent cottages toward the druids' compound. A sack rubs uncomfortably on my back, and my harp inside digs into my shoulder. I can't leave without it, though, as it is the only way I can think of to earn my bread.

The bright moon illuminates one nodding guard in front of the door to a thatched windowless hut. I lower my sack to the ground and approach the man on soundless feet. I'm within three steps when he finally startles awake and surges to his feet. I close the distance and grab any lauvan I can reach, especially near his throat. As I hoped, his yell for help is no more than a hoarse whisper.

He is quick and lunges for me to pin me to the ground. I

twist in his grasp, but he holds me tightly with his weight. I thrust my fingers into his strands in a panic, desperate to release myself from my trap.

To my intense relief and surprise, the man's eyes roll back, and he slumps onto me. I push him off with distaste and rise with shaking legs.

The door of the hut is latched shut on the outside. When I swing it open, the darkness within moves.

"Who is there?" a ragged voice whispers.

"Do you want to die tomorrow?" I whisper back. "If not, the door is open. Make your escape. I am."

The slave emerges. He's a big man, but too thin for his frame. He shivers in his dirty woolen tunic and glances around the clearing with the eyes of a hunted animal.

I wrestle the guard out of his coat and hand it to the slave. A loaf of bread from my bag also makes its way into his hands.

"I'm going east, to find a ship to Britain," I say. "You're welcome to accompany me if you wish. Or go your own way."

The man nods slowly, his face a mess of expressions. Fear, curiosity, confusion, and hope play in his eyes.

"I will come with you, if you will have me."

I grin and pat him on the shoulder.

"Come. On to our next adventure."

CHAPTER IX

It's a beautiful afternoon, all blue skies and brisk breezes, so I decide to do my thinking and planning from a mountaintop. Nothing opens my mind more freely than immersion in the forest and a deep grounding with the Earth. I could be doing something more concrete toward my goal of stopping human sacrifice, but starting out with a solid plan is important.

I can't lie to myself after all these years—I know myself too well. This is procrastination, pure and simple. I want answers to my questions, but I can't have the answers I seek, not at the cost of an innocent. But to know the central mystery of my life...

One afternoon of thought won't hurt. Potestas won't move that quickly. I slide into my car, parked near the cupcake shop/headquarters of doom, but before I can turn the ignition, my phone rings.

"Hello?" I say.

"Hola, Merlo," says Alejandro. "Did you have your meeting? What happened?"

"Are you free now to come for a hike? I can tell you all about it."

"Si, of course. I'm at home."

"I'll be there in ten."

Alejandro waits on the sidewalk when I pull up to the curb, and he hops in.

"Where are we going?" he asks. His bright eyes gaze at me in question. I nod toward the mountains.

"I thought we'd try Mount Seymour today. There isn't enough time to go any further afield."

"Will there be views?"

"A few. Not quite as spectacular as Cypress mountain."

"But fewer crazy spirit-men."

"Yes. Hopefully."

I ask Alejandro about his new apartment and his job, and both topics elicit enthusiasm. It's not until we reach the highway that Alejandro turns the conversation.

"But Merlo, you haven't told me about your meeting. What happened at Potestas?"

I switch gears to pass a moving truck.

"Not much. Oh, except for the news that the ceremony will require a human sacrifice."

Alejandro's eyes grow as round as coins.

"What? And everyone is okay with that?"

"March's influence is greater than I supposed. There was hardly a murmur at the news, and no one stepped forward to protest. Indeed, most simply looked excited by the prospect of spirit connection, without a thought for the poor unfortunate who will fuel the process."

Alejandro sits back and digests the information. His forest-green lauvan spasm with discomfort.

"Who will it be?"

"I'm not certain. From what I could gather, they are currently searching for someone with a 'strong aura.'"

"What does that mean?"

"Who knows? But it lends more urgency to my mission to relieve Potestas of the grail."

"Our mission," Alejandro says in a firm tone. "I want this done, too, and I can help."

I flash him a grateful smile.

"Thanks, Alejandro. I won't forget."

I don't tell him about my contact with the earth spirits. I've been keeping secrets for so many centuries that laying my actions bare all at once doesn't feel natural. And my desire to know more, to let the ceremony continue so that I can speak with the successor—well, I can't imagine how well Alejandro might take that. How could he understand my desire to know? He is so young, and so pure-of-heart. There would never be a question in his mind. I don't want to tarnish my image in his eyes, not yet. I'm sure that will come soon enough.

We drive in silence for a few minutes. After we span the bridge that crosses Burrard Inlet, I exit northeast toward the mountain.

"Do you hike often?" Alejandro breaks the thoughtful silence.

"Fairly often. I think best surrounded by trees, with solid rock under my feet. I like to plug into the lauvan cables while I'm there, too. It's good to keep tabs on the world."

"What does 'plugging in' mean?" Alejandro asks.

"If I touch a lauvan cable, I can send my mind along its length and see if anything is out of place." I rub my chin while I try to explain. "I don't see, per se, it's more of a sensation. And it's a rush."

"How far can you go like that?" Alejandro leans forward in his interest.

"A good ways. From here, I could likely travel as far as Alberta before the sensation grew too faint. I feel less and less connected to my body the further I go, so I don't push it. I'm not curious enough to test that boundary."

"I wish I could try it," says Alejandro with a wistful expression. I shrug.

"There's no one else who can. No one I've met, anyway." Not even the spirits seem to know anyone like me, and they knew of me. The thought depresses me. It's hard when a hope dies, faint as it might be. It was always a possibility that there were others like me, but with the spirits' question that hope has fizzled to nothing.

My mood must show on my face, because Alejandro's next words are in a comforting tone.

"Sometimes what you don't have is what you don't need, and what you have is what you should."

"Well said, Alejandro." Echoes of the past drift through my mind. Arthur used to say something similar. "Someone wise once told me the same thing. Long ago. It's still true, all these years later."

Alejandro nods but says nothing. The car climbs up the mountain road, winding back and forth, ever upward, until we arrive at a parking lot. I pull into a spot and stop the car.

"This will do. We can hike from here," I say. "It's a half-hour walk to the nearest cable. Are you ready?"

"Always," says Alejandro. "Lead the way."

The main trail is well-groomed, but we soon take a little-used path that branches off the main one. Rocks and roots abound, and I am glad of my sturdy hiking boots. Alejandro slips in his running shoes but gamely presses on. Soon, neither of us has much breath for talking, and Alejandro's face registers relief when I halt at a clearing in the woods.

"Time for a break?" he pants. I shake my head.

"No, we're here. Behold, a lauvan cable lies before you." At Alejandro's perplexed peering, I chuckle. "Never mind. Sit on that log and have a rest while I check the cable."

Alejandro sinks gratefully onto the felled tree, and I approach the cable. It glitters and glistens with a light not of the sun. Thousands of strands lie bundled together in a long mass that reaches from one end of the clearing to the other and disappears into the trees on either end. The bundle rises to the height of my chest, and its entire surface is alive with slowly wriggling lauvan. Every shade of brown imaginable is represented in its depths, but predominant is a silvery-brown. The ground almost hums with the many strands that link to the cable.

When I am close enough, I reach out my hands and take a few deep breaths before I plunge them into the writhing mass. My body seizes with sensation, and my head whips back in blissful agony. I allow myself a few moments to wallow in the feeling but soon control myself. Alejandro is watching, and I have things to do.

Gradually, I close my eyes and allow my conscious to flow down my arms and into the cable. I feel distinctly separate from my body, with only a frail point of connection to tether me. The lauvan stream in one direction, and while I could fight the flow, I have no reason to today, so I follow the cable northwest.

All is as expected, and my mind floats with the strands in a pleasant, meandering way. I travel down the mountain, into a valley, and across a river. Around the next mountain, a faint tingling travels through my conscious. Something is different about the center ahead of me, the place where multiple cables converge, but I don't know what. It's nothing as terrible as the sickness at Wallerton when the spirits attempted to erupt a dormant volcano. It's strange, but not truly concerning.

I've been away from my body for long enough, and the connection draws my mind back along the cable when I let it. When I arrive at my body, my eyes open and I stretch.

"How long was I gone?" I ask. It's difficult to tell time in the cables, especially without the cues my body provides.

"Maybe twenty minutes? I lost track." Alejandro has made himself comfortable with the log as a pillow and his running shoes kicked off. His face beams with contentment under the summer sun. He closes his eyes again and puts his hands behind his head. "Find anything interesting?"

"A slight disturbance to the west, but nothing much to worry about. Perhaps some instability left over from an earthquake. All is well here. No imminent natural disasters that I could sense."

"Good," Alejandro says in a lazy tone. I walk over and prod his ribs with the toe of my boot. He grimaces. "What was that for?"

"Come on, lazybones. The best views are still another half-hour away. I thought you came for a hike?"

"You're the one who stopped partway through," he grumbles, but he takes my offered hand and hauls himself up.

We continue along our little-known path, and the dense coniferous forest eventually opens to a slope of rocky scree. A dusty valley of green trees spreads below our feet, and other mountains loom across the way. There's a light haze over the scene from the last of the night's moisture evaporating off the trees, but the brilliant sun makes short work of it.

Alejandro stops beside me and breathes deeply then stretches his arms out as if to embrace the view.

"Beautiful. Makes me glad to be alive."

I smile and open my mouth to reply, but a rumbling sound makes me pause. I look around to spot the source of the noise. To our left, a dozen paces up the gravely embankment, the hillside shifts. The entire rocky ground flows with ever-increasing velocity until individual stones roll and kick upward in chaotic patterns. The mass rumbles down, straight toward us.

I go to grab Alejandro's arm, but he's already leaping back into the safety of the trees. The rockslide surges past us with a roar. It doesn't pause until a small hill funnels the rocks into a valley, a hundred paces below us where they lose momentum and come to a dusty, grinding standstill.

We watch in silence until the last of the rocks settles and quiet reigns once more. I look at Alejandro.

"I think I've had enough hiking for today. Ready to head

back?"

"You took the words right out of my mouth," he says with relief. "Views are overrated, anyway. Seen one, seen them all."

I laugh and follow him back the way we came. The trees feel protective and safe after our rockslide scare. I've never heard of a slide on Mount Seymour before. It has too many visitors not to be strictly monitored for safety.

A figure appears on the path ahead of us. He's dressed for hiking with sturdy boots, rugged pants, and a trim backpack. He greets us.

"Great day to get out of the city."

"Watch yourself up there." I point behind us. "We narrowly missed a rockfall. At the viewpoint, where it opens up."

"Thanks for the warning." The man takes a water bottle from a side pouch on his pack and squirts it into his mouth. "Seems like there's a lot of that going around."

"How so?"

"Didn't you hear about the big slide at Whistler? Just about took out some mountain bikers. Maybe the conditions are right for loose ground, I don't know. Anyway." He puts his water bottle back. "Enjoy the rest of your walk."

He gives us a friendly wave then disappears up the path. I turn to Alejandro.

"Strange. I wonder if the disturbance in the cable is related. Or perhaps forcing the two phenomena together is grasping at coincidences."

"Speaking of together," Alejandro says, his mind clearly elsewhere. "Jen wants to know if you and Minnie want to go for dinner at Flourish tonight. I want to meet her."

"I'll check with Minnie," I say, but in my head, I've already said yes. I like to bring the disparate parts of my life together. I spend too much time hiding and keeping secrets to willingly accept division. And the evening is long—there will be plenty of time for friends and for romance.

Minnie slides her arm through mine before we reach the restaurant doors. It's a rooftop patio that serves tapas and high-priced drinks. Jen picked it—coming from a well-off family sometimes makes her blind to expense—but Alejandro, even with his ESL teacher's wage, is still in the early, besotted stage of his relationship with Jen and didn't protest. Minnie squeezes my arm.

"This is a little weird," she says to me quietly. "I mean, I know Jen through her cousin. I know her family, she's met me a bunch of times."

"And that will make conversation all the smoother," I say. "You won't have to worry about boring small talk. You can jump right in. Jen adores gossiping. Surely you've heard something juicy lately?"

Minnie nudges me with her shoulder and laughs.

"I guess you're right. Still, it's hard not to expect judgement. For dating a former client. I know I need to get over that."

"Trust me, you won't get any judgement from Jen. I might." I grin at Minnie, who kisses my cheek. She pulls back to evaluate my reaction.

"What was that for?" I ask. Not that I mind, but I hadn't realized we were at that stage of easy intimacy.

"I felt like it," she says. "Come on, they're probably waiting. We're a bit late."

"I'm curious to see whether they are on time or not." I open the door for Minnie. She enters, and I follow her into a small foyer that leads to a wide staircase with a hostess desk at the top. "Alejandro has a Latin flexibility with time, and Jen is quite the opposite."

Minnie climbs the stairs and gazes around the open-air patio at the top. She waves at someone near the edge of the roof.

"Jen prevailed," she says. "I haven't met your friend Alejandro yet, but I can imagine Jen being the more forceful one in a relationship."

I chuckle and take Minnie's hand to pull her toward my friends.

"Too true."

The patio overlooks English Bay, and the low sun glances off the calm waters with a gleaming bronze light. Tankers and sailboats alike cleave the ocean on their paths. Alejandro stands when we arrive at the table and shakes Minnie's hand.

"I'm Alejandro. So good to meet you." His thick hair is somewhat tamed, and he looks comfortable in a short-sleeved buttoned shirt. No, he looks more than comfortable—he looks blissful. The source of his bliss stands also and gives Minnie a hug.

"Hi, Minnie," says Jen. "It's great to see you again. I hope you guys like shrimp—we ordered our first tapas already."

As I hoped, conversation is easy and fluid. We touch on subjects ranging from sightseeing to soccer to surfing—apparently, Minnie is an accomplished surfer. It's been a long time since I felt this comfortable chatting with good friends. Tapas come and go, drinks flow, and with every story Minnie tells about herself—her move to Vancouver, her near-miss with a shark while surfing in Hawaii, her favorite novel—another lauvan bond forms between us. A navy-blue strand sinuously travels through the air to meet my waiting chocolate brown thread, and they twist together to form another connection.

After a couple of quick hours, Minnie excuses herself from the table.

"Powder room," she says. "I'll be right back."

She smiles at me when she leaves, and I can't help but return my own. When I look back at the others, Jen looks at me with raised eyebrows.

"Wow, Merry. I didn't know you were capable of it." She waves her hand. "Well, obviously, you told me you had fourteen wives or whatever, but I've never seen the evidence."

"Evidence of what?" What is she trying to say?

She tsks.

"Oh, Merry. You're so in love." She smiles at me, then exchanges a complicit look with Alejandro. He nods.

"It's true," he says. "You're, what's the word? Starts with 's.'"

"Smitten?" Jen says.

"Yes, smitten."

They both turn back to me with smug expressions on their faces. I shake my head.

"No, of course I'm not. She's a pleasant companion for the moment, nothing more."

"Stop fooling yourself, Merry," Jen says. "A blind person could see it. You're head over heels."

I stare at her. The noise of the restaurant dulls to an indecipherable roar in my ears. Surely not. I was careful. I only wanted someone to spend time with. I don't want love. I can't handle any more.

I look at the cloud of lauvan that surrounds me. It stretches past my shoulders, almost as far as my arm-span. At the edges, it is so far away from my body that it fades into transparency. My breath comes more quickly. I'm already unraveling. What would happen with one more love lost? Would my strands all disappear into nothing? Would I be gone forever?

Jen says something, her face alarmed, but the words don't register. I can't let this continue, no further than it already has. I have to break it off with Minnie. There's no other way.

I push back from the table. The others' faces are startled, but I can't force words out of my constricted throat. My feet take me blindly to the stairs, where I run down two steps at a time and push through the glass door at the bottom onto the street. There is a park opposite, only a tiny patch of grass, but blessedly free of people. I race across the street to a chorus of honks and skid to my knees on the grass.

Feverishly, I grasp the blue and brown lauvan that connect me with Minnie. There are so many connections. How did I ignore this? How did I let it go this far? Was I too "smitten" to read the warning signs? I pluck the first connection free of the bundle, hold it between both hands, and pull hard.

The lauvan break with a snap, and I gasp with pain. A sharp jab rips into me, deep in my chest, and leaves an ache near my heart that is too familiar. But it is better to finish this now and suffer a minor pain than to disintegrate in forty years. I break another, and the pain takes my breath away. Another, and I bend over, clutching both hands to my chest.

"Merry! What are you doing?"

Jen sprints across the grass toward me. Her form is blurry through my streaming eyes. She kneels before me and grabs my shoulders roughly.

"I'm breaking the connection," I gasp. "I can't do this again. I can't love another woman, not like that. I won't survive."

I grit my teeth and reach for the next lauvan strand. Jen stops me with her hands on mine.

"Stop it, Merry. You're hurting yourself. And you're hurting Minnie, too. She's doubled over in the restaurant, you know."

I stare at the ground, undecided.

"It won't last long," I say finally. "Not for her. She will heal and find someone else. Momentary pain, long-term benefit."

"No," Jen says, her voice harsh. "I won't stand by and watch you hurt both of you. And you can't give up on love, not yet. You don't know that you can't handle it. It's all conjecture. And what about the years of joy being with someone can bring? Doesn't that count for anything?"

I am silent for a long while, although I don't try to break another connection. After Jen's words, I don't have the energy. She can't understand this situation, not from my point of view. Who could? One would think that I would be used to loss by now, but it's quite the opposite.

But Jen does have a point, if not the one she intended. What's the point of causing all this immediate pain, when the lauvan strands will fade on their own, given enough time?

"All right," I say. My voice sounds defeated, even to my ears. "I won't break them."

Jen looks like she wants to give me a hug but is held back by something.

"Let's go back to dinner." She stands and holds out her hand. I take it and haul myself up. Sometimes, I feel the weight of every one of my fifteen hundred-odd years. "They'll be wondering where we went."

Minnie is pale but composed when we approach the table. Alejandro looks back and forth between Jen and me but doesn't dare to inquire further when Jen shakes her head.

"I heard you had a rough spell," I say to Minnie. "Would you like me to take you home?"

"I think that would be wise," she says quietly then turns to Jen and Alejandro. "Thanks for a lovely evening."

Jen hugs Minnie tightly.

"See you soon, Minnie."

Minnie and I are quiet on the way to the car. I don't know where to begin and rehearse what to say to her before we part ways forever. I sneak a few glances at Minnie, and every time I do her face is solemn and her lauvan swirl in confusion and lingering pain. I wince. I was too hasty when I tried to rip us apart, I see that now. The long, slow method of separation will have to suffice, days and weeks of missing and longing until one by one the lauvan that connect us drift apart from each other and the yearning grows distant. Never forgotten, only dulled over time.

It's not until we're in the car and halfway to Minnie's apartment that I break the silence.

"Are you feeling all right?"

She grimaces and rubs her chest.

"I'll survive. I don't know what that was about. I'd better go to the clinic in the morning, get it checked out."

I nod absently, then grip the steering wheel with tight fingers.

"Minnie. I don't think we should see each other anymore."

There, it's out. Those are words that are hard to take back. Minnie's jaw drops.

"What? Why?" When I don't respond immediately, she says, "Is this because of the client thing? Because I thought you didn't care."

"I don't."

"Then what?" Minnie's eyes bore into the side of my head, but I keep my eyes on the road. "Is it the voices you were hearing last week? What's going on? I can handle whatever you throw at me." She gives me a beat to respond. I leave only

68

silence. She says in exasperation, "Do you think you're protecting me?"

I shake my head. I would laugh if my heart didn't ache so much.

"No, you have it wrong. Don't paint me as some selfless man, too noble to want to cause you hurt. The reality is that I'm protecting myself."

"From what?" she says, repressed emotion sharpening her voice.

"I've fallen in love with you, Minnie Dilleck," I say. Minnie's breath hitches. I turn left and pull over in front of her apartment building. "I'm in love, and I can't do it. Not again. I can't lose someone else. I need to stop this before it's too late, before I sink too deep into us." I finally look at Minnie, and my jaw tightens at the confusion and hurt in her eyes. Her lauvan swirl and spasm with uncertainty. "I'm sorry."

Minnie searches my face. The silence stretches like taffy.

"I guess this is it," she says finally. The words are a question, and her eyes blink away tears that she won't let fall.

"Yes," I whisper.

Minnie picks up her purse from the floor of the car and puts her hand on the door handle. She turns to face me once more.

"Call me when you change your mind," she says. Her voice is calm again, concealing the torrent of emotion that her strands can't hide. "I understand where your sentiments are probably coming from, but you can't live in isolation forever. As your former psychologist and your friend, I ask you to think carefully before you push me away for good."

One last look, and Minnie steps out of the car and closes the door. She walks to her building and doesn't look back.

The weight of my decision crushes my shoulders until I could sink into my steering wheel and never peel myself off. What have I done? What could I have done differently?

Nothing, is what. There was no way out of this that didn't involve pain. Not for the first time, I wonder why I'm still here on this Earth.

I drive home in a daze, scarcely noticing where I'm going. By luck or by habit I find myself in the parking lot of my building and sit for a moment in the cooling car. The white noise of fans outside my car window muffles my thoughts, the thoughts that swirl in a fog against the confines of my mind.

Out of habit, again, I open the door and stumble my way to the elevator, and from there to my apartment. My fingers pull off my shirt and unbutton my pants, then I flop onto my bed. I don't plan to leave it for a while. The fog of thoughts beat against my skull until I force myself into a trance, which eventually becomes sleep. Not that my dreams are any less painful, but they are an old pain, not the jagged, fresh wounds of today.

CHAPTER X

Dreaming

Rain pelts the windows, smothering their floor-to-ceiling lengths with a smear of wetness. The constant noise grates at my nerves even through the fog of my grief, and thick velvet curtains barely dampen the sound. I lean against the windowsill and stare sightlessly across my estate. Rolling green lawns gleam with emerald damp under the gray skies, and the orchard's blossoms are being slowly beaten away by the rain. Fruit will be scarce this year. This pains me—the pippin apples were Celeste's favorite.

But she's gone now. What does it matter if no fruit set this year? Celeste can't taste apples from the grave.

There is a knock at the door of my chamber. My manservant Frederick opens the door and bows.

"My lord?" he says.

"What?" I growl.

"The post has arrived. There is a letter from your solicitor, Mr. Nicholson. I took the liberty of opening it, as you instructed."

"Then why are you bothering me with the contents? That was the sole purpose of my instruction, so you need not come to me."

He bows but is not dissuaded.

"Your properties in Suffolk require an urgent decision."

I hold up my hand, and he stops speaking.

"Let Mr. Nicholson decide. I care not. I leave the matter in his eminently capable hands, and you may say as much when you write." I turn back to the window with disinterest.

"The post also included three invitations to dinner parties in the neighborhood, one hosted by Lady Stanton herself."

"I have no desire to engage in flippant conversation about the gossip from Bath or the latest in bonnet fashion. Kindly decline, as you have been requested before." I put some iron in my words, and he looks slightly abashed.

"One final missive—summons to court by the Prince Regent—"

"Enough!" I roar. "Leave at once, sirrah!"

He bows and backs out swiftly. I sag against the wall, by turns annoyed and ashamed at my outburst. If I had visions that being a titled noble in Regency-era England would allow me to wallow in my grief in peace, I was sorely mistaken.

Celeste would have laughed me out of my misery. We moved to England ten years ago, and this time around she styled herself as an eccentric dowager to the world, doting to her young nephew Lord Meryton, and full of sharp-edged wisdom to the rest. She ruled the neighborhood with a lace-cuffed fist, and we gleefully terrorized all the best parties in town during the season. My stomach aches with the intensity of my longing for Celeste, and I turn from the window to approach my four-poster bed. We were together for over fifty years. Perhaps I can lose myself in dreams.

Scarcely half an hour passes before I hear the crunch of wheels on gravel. Who has come to visit me? I force myself out of bed, stumble to the door, and swing it open.

"No visitors!" I bellow, then slam the door for good measure. If that doesn't convince Frederick that I don't wish to be disturbed, then I don't know what will. I could sack him, I suppose. I throw myself on the bed, but my rest is disturbed once more. My mouth twists in a snarl, and my fingers twitch in their desire to grasp lauvan.

My door bursts open, and I shrink at the truly formidable sight. Mrs. Jeanine Landon, young wife of the late Mr. Landon and my longtime friend, stands at the threshold. Her chestnut

72

ringlets are tightly curled as if they dare not stray. Her muslin gown is impeccable despite the downpour, and I can only suppose she insisted on multiple umbrellas on her trip from carriage to hall. Her yellow lauvan are taut with her resolve and are the only source of sunshine in the room. Her pert nose wrinkles in distaste at my unaired chamber and slovenly appearance.

"Lord Meryton." It's not a question, merely a demand for my attention. "You have isolated yourself in your country home for two months—two months!—and caused all manner of disturbance in town. I had to suffer through three of Mrs. Bailey's whist parties on my own, and I'm certain you'll agree that I cannot bear a fourth." She sighs and her lauvan relax slightly. "I understand that you mourn deeply for your aunt. She was a kind soul, and I admired her immensely. But you cannot renounce all society forever. You have mourned for longer than is respectable for a relation of that kind, and now it is time to be yourself once more."

Jeanine gives me a sharp nod after her little speech and adjusts her pristine white gloves with determined tugs. I gaze at her with frustration and something else. It has been so long since I've felt amusement that I hardly recognize the sensation.

"You have come all this way to scold sense into me?"

She tilts her chin up.

"I have. And I won't take no for an answer. Frederick?" She says this last in a louder voice, and Frederick leaps around the corner and bows. He must have been waiting beside the door. I scowl at him, but it is halfhearted, and I know he can tell, for his somber face twitches with amusement. "Please prepare Lord Meryton to take tea with me." She looks me up and down. "Do your best."

He barely hides his grin as he approaches me with a comb. "Yes, my lady."

I sit up and resign myself to Frederick's ministrations.

When I enter the parlor an hour later, Jeanine looks me over with approval from her perch on the settee.

"You are much improved, Lord Meryton. While the beard lent you a certain rakish air, you are far handsomer without it. And far more reputable."

"In appearance, I suppose." I sink onto the chair opposite with a sigh. I have been inactive for so long that even my ablutions tire me. Jeanine raises an eyebrow.

"Indeed."

My butler Jenson approaches with the tea and assorted refreshments. Jeanine leans forward to pour, and my throat constricts. When Celeste was alive, pouring the tea was always her duty and her pleasure in this house. When Jeanine passes me a cup, I have a hard time croaking out thanks. A sharp eye tells me my emotion is not unnoticed.

"I know you were close with your aunt," Jeanine says gently. "So close, that, I sometimes doubt that she was your aunt at all."

My hands are motionless on my tea cup and my eyes widen involuntarily. What does she think she knows?

"You may keep your secrets, Lord Meryton," she says with a dainty sip of her tea. "I have no desire to pry. I have endless curiosity, of course." She smiles impishly. "But you need not divulge. However, to the world, your mourning has carried on for too long. It is unseemly, and there is much talk of your self-imposed hermitage."

"Let them talk," I say. "I care not."

"You may not care for your reputation, but someone must," she says sharply. "That is why I have sent replies of acceptance to your invitations. Two dinner parties and a tea this week, if I am not mistaken."

"I will not go," I say. What right had Jeanine to order me

74

about like one of her maids? "I have no wish to murmur insipid pleasantries to the matrons or speak of shooting with the men. I especially am not inclined to make love to their empty-headed daughters. I will not go."

"You will. You will attend every one, and you will act as befits a young man grieving for an aunt—with some solemnity, but with lightheartedness also."

I close my eyes. The pain of Celeste's passing is still so raw. How can I hide that? Why should I?

"You will go," Jeanine repeats. "And I will go with you, to every function. I will stay at your side, and we will come through the other side of your grief." She leans forward, and I meet her earnest eyes, filled with compassion. "Closing yourself off from the world will not allow you to heal. Let me help you."

Slowly, I nod. She is right, of course. Shutting myself away is all I can manage when my lover dies, but it never helps. I never know how to wake myself up from my misery, and it gets harder every time. Jeanine's methods might aggravate, but I cannot deny they work. I am lucky to have a friend such as she.

CHAPTER XI

My phone awakens me in the morning, but I don't bother reaching for it, instead slipping back into fragmented dreams. Hours later, it rings again. I'm too far gone in my fog to be annoyed, or even curious, so I reach for it on my bedside table and check the screen. Unread texts, unanswered calls—I don't care. I turn the phone off and lay back down.

When I'm not sleeping, I force myself into a trance state. I hate this. I hate hurting Minnie. I hate the terrible ache in my chest. I hate that it reminds me of every loss I've had to endure, every memory welling up from the recesses of my mind to torment me. In the past, I've tried distractions to keep myself busy, but it doesn't work and it's far too much effort in my current state. I don't bother anymore. It's simpler to crawl into my proverbial cave until the pain isn't as raw.

My stomach eventually rebels, and I shuffle into the kitchen to shove bread into my mouth but return to bed once the hole is filled. Day fades to night and sleep follows trance. At least my lauvan are still attached to my body. I did something right. Whatever loss I feel now is nothing compared to what would happen had I stayed with Minnie, had we lived a full lifetime together. I saved myself from heartbreak, possibly from death itself.

So why can't I shake this pain-filled lethargy?

Sun streams in my window the next morning, but I don't want to see it. I roll onto my stomach and bury my head in my pillow. My stomach rumbles, but I ignore it. I've suffered worse hunger pangs. I'd rather be lost in my fog than bother to satisfy my body's needs. Perhaps later I will stir myself.

There is a knock at the door. I don't move. If I'm lucky, the knocker will go away.

I'm not lucky. There is a scuffing sound of the door sweep across the floor, then a click as the door closes.

"Merry?" Jen calls out. "Are you home?"

I don't bother to reply. She'll find me soon enough. Footsteps pad along the carpet until her voice speaks from the door of my bedroom.

"Merry. What are you doing still in bed? Don't you have class this morning?"

I grunt but don't offer anything more coherent.

"You weren't returning my texts or calls. I was worried about you after the other night. Are you okay?" She kneels beside the bed to look at my face. Hers shows a mixture of exasperation, concern, and a hint of something else. Wariness, perhaps?

"I don't want to see anybody," I mumble. "I want to stay in bed."

Jen frowns at me.

"Have you been here since dinner the other night?"

I shrug in reply. Jen releases a little laugh of incredulity then shakes her head.

"What is it, Merry? You can tell me. What on Earth would possess you to stop your life like this?"

"I broke it off with Minnie," I say, and Jen's face falls. "I was falling in love. I couldn't handle it." I close my eyes to hint to Jen to leave me alone. She is silent for only a moment.

"Now you're moping in bed in response?"

"Works for me."

"How many centuries old are you, and you act like an emo teenager?" The exasperation is back, along with a thread of fondness. That's much better than the wary tone from earlier.

"Sometimes the youth have it right."

"Not this time." Jen stands and turns on a no-nonsense voice. "You're getting up, showering, eating a solid breakfast, and going to work. Got it? Wallowing won't help one bit. Come on, it's time."

Before I can growl my displeasure, Jen yanks the covers off the bed. She shrieks.

"Merry! Put some pants on!" There's a scuffling on the floor, then my jeans land across my naked bottom. "Honestly. A little warning next time," she mutters as she marches from the room.

"It's just a bit of skin," I say to her retreating back. "I picked up the habit early on—all Saxons slept naked—and I never quit."

"It's the twenty-first century, Merry," she yells from the kitchen over the sound of running water. "Honestly. Check a calendar."

My annoyance at Jen's meddling is the first emotion that has cut through the fog in the past day and a half. That, along with the rush of cool air over my naked skin, serves to galvanize me into action. I grumble all the way to the bathroom, but when hot water hits my face and steam rises in the shower, my annoyance with Jen battles with gratitude that she is there to pull me out of my funk. Usually, when I battle my melancholy, it's because someone has died and left me. This time, I am not alone.

I emerge from the shower, feeling renewed. The ache in my chest from the loss of Minnie from my life is still present but cushioned by Jen's presence. I open the bathroom door to the smell of fresh coffee and toast.

"It's all I could find in your empty fridge," Jen says when I enter the kitchen, tousling my hair with my fingers to dry it. "Were you planning to starve yourself?"

"The glories of the modern world include delivery food."

"But then you might have to put on pants."

"Is that truly a requirement?" I raise an eyebrow, and Jen

smacks my arm. "With enough extra cash, anything is permissible."

"We're not talking about this anymore." Jen shoves a plate of toast and a full mug at me. "Here, eat this."

I wolf down the toast to the delight of my hungry stomach. Jen sips her coffee while she waits for me to stop inhaling my food.

"Merry. I don't know if you forgot while you were lounging on your bed for the last two days, but we still have a grail to find and an evil plan to stop. Any ideas?"

"It's not at Potestas headquarters." I swallow the last of my toast and lean back in my chair. "I checked. There are many places it could be, but the most likely is in March's safe, in her house."

"How are we going to get it?"

"We need two things: the location of March's house—"

"I can figure that out," Jen says with a decisive nod.

"And the key to the safe, from around March's wrist," I finish.

"How on Earth are we going to get that?" Jen's face scrunches with disappointment and concern. An idea blossoms in my mind, and I smile slowly.

"I have an idea."

"What?" Jen says, then she holds up her hand. Her lauvan tense with nervousness. "Wait, I don't want to know."

I sip my coffee and look at Jen as she takes her plate to the kitchen. What does she mean by that comment? What does she think I plan to do? Ever since she asked me how many people I've killed, she has been tip-toeing around me, not asking her endless questions, not wanting to know details about plans. Is she frightened of me? How can I reassure her when I might be the problem?

Jen leaves soon after, but not before she watches me put my car keys and wallet in my pocket and extracts a promise from me that I'll go to work today.

It does feel good to move, although every time my eye catches Minnie's lauvan reaching out from my center, my gut clenches. I turn on my music loudly in the car to drown out my thoughts, and Chopin blasts through the speakers.

The class looks surprised to see me after my absence yesterday. I don't bother to explain. They can surmise what they like.

"Talk to me about Alexander Pope's *An Essay on Man*, Epistle Two. Taylor, read the first stanza, please."

Taylor looks nonplussed at being called upon so quickly, but I don't feel like lecturing today. The students can do the work. They must sense that I am in no mood to be trifled with, and most sit up straight. The young woman I called upon clears her throat before she speaks.

"Know then thyself, presume not God to scan; the proper study of mankind is man. Plac'd on this isthmus of a middle state, a being darkly wise, and rudely great: with too much knowledge for the sceptic side, with too much weakness for the stoic's pride, he hangs between; in doubt to act, or rest; in doubt to deem himself a god, or beast; in doubt his mind or body to prefer; born but to die, and reas'ning but to err; alike in ignorance, his reason such, whether he thinks too little, or too much: chaos of thought and passion, all confus'd; still by himself abus'd, or disabus'd; created half to rise, and half to fall; great lord of all things, yet a prey to all; sole judge of truth, in endless error hurl'd: the glory, jest, and riddle of the world!"

The reading was lackluster, as expected, but I didn't have

to do it.

"Let's hear your thoughts on what Pope means when he says, 'The proper study of mankind is man,'" I say.

A few raise their hands. I point to one at random, a young man with a shock of curly brown hair.

"Is he saying that humans shouldn't presume to question God, but they should study themselves to get answers about the world?"

"With conviction, people," I say. "Own your opinion. Goodness knows you're too young to have one but have some confidence all the same. Yes, that's correct. What else?"

I try to keep my attitude in check while we discuss Pope's poetry and the humanism infused in it, but it's a trial. There is one young woman in the back whose hair is the exact chestnut brown shade of Minnie's, and it distracts me with a pang in my chest every time my eyes pass her head. Another student sips from a travel mug and I am reminded of the grail, still hidden from me.

The student puts down her mug and adjusts her bracelet. She is close enough to the front that the engraving on the metal band is visible. It's a stylized mountain. I would have disregarded it, except for the thick cover of brown lauvan that swirl around it and almost obscure the mountain from my view. My breath catches and I look at her face, but she writes in her notebook and doesn't look at me.

How many Potestas members are there, that I can come across one at random in my class? Or, a chilling thought: is she planted here to watch me? I avoid unnecessary paranoia, but it might be warranted with March. I will have to watch my back.

"Dr. Lytton?" A student says tentatively from the front. The class gazes at me with curiosity. Some hide snickers behind their hands, but I am respected enough that outright laughter would never occur. I shake my head.

"That's enough for today. Make sure your papers are ready for me next class. And a helpful hint: include some of our discussion today."

A few students look like they wish to speak with me, but I sweep out of the room before they can corner me. I have a plan to take the key from March, and I must complete it tonight. Time is running out.

CHAPTER XII

Back in my office, I open the window to get rid of the stuffy air and pull out my phone. The photos of the list of Potestas members are still there, and I send the photos to my printer. A minute later, I grab a pen and the pages and start crossing off names. I'm looking for a man, so all female names get scratched out. March has helpfully included birthdates, so every man under forty-five doesn't make the cut. That leaves me with six names. I plug each into a search engine and pull up the results.

Two of the names don't return any consistent results, so I scratch them off my list. The other four have potential. Jeremy Barnum is a realtor with a winning smile. Stephen Vlad runs a smoke shop in East Van and favors tie-dye shirts. Connor Luther's main hobby is running, as far as I can tell, and his photos invariably show him sweating in small shorts. Valencio Lopez is a photographer whose serious expression is only captured in one picture despite hundreds of his photos being online.

I grab the best photo of each, along with a quick description of each man, and send Jen an email marked URGENT.

If you were a fifty-something woman with a strong business mind and a spiritual bent, who would you find the most attractive?

I have a good idea, but it never hurts to get a woman's opinion. I'm often surprised.

Five minutes later, I have my answer.

Jeremy Barnum, hands down. What on Earth do you have planned?

I reply with a smiley face and nothing else. She'll figure it out. The only way to get close to March—short of attacking her and wrenching the bracelet off her, which would blow my cover, putting aside the ethics—is to take her on a date.

Jeremy Barnum has an office in Kitsilano, so I phone to find out his plans for tonight.

"Haven Realty," a woman's voice answers.

"Hello," I say in a cheery British accent. "Looking for Jeremy Barnum. Do you know, is he in?"

"I'm sorry, you've just missed him," she says. "Can I take a message?"

"It's just, I'm leaving tomorrow, and I really wanted to speak with him before I go. My daughter, she lives here, she's looking for a new house and asked me to call the realtor. Wouldn't you know it, I forgot until right now. She'll be livid. You don't know where I could find him? Is he showing a house?"

"He's showing a house currently, yes," she says in a regretful tone. "But I don't think you'll catch him before he finishes for the day. He has the evening booked off for personal errands. But let me take your name and number and I will have him call you first thing in the morning. Will that work? When does your flight leave?"

"That will be wonderful, thanks." I rattle off a false phone number and hang up.

It's possible that Jeremy is running errands, but with an ex-wife and kids that live out of town, according to his unprotected social media account, my bet is a Potestas visit tonight. He could be watching television or on a date, but Potestas members tend to treat headquarters as their home-away-from-home. I'll go and watch him, learn his habits, and when he leaves, I'll make my move.

I grab a quick burger from the food court on campus—an anemic thing, but it will do for sustenance—and drive to Sweet Thing. The cupcake shop closes early, and chairs are piled on tables in the unlit store. The door is open, as always, and I slide inside and enter the secret door in the kitchen.

A low hum of chatting greets my ears. Three people are playing a board game on a nearby coffee table, and the kitchen houses pizza boxes and happily munching members. I recognize Jeremy Barnum in the kitchen. His tie is loosened, and his sleeves are rolled up. He laughs with a middle-aged woman dressed in a blouse and pencil skirt and uses his slice of pizza to punctuate his words.

I sit on an unoccupied couch and pull out a notebook and pen. I have nothing I need to jot down, but it's a cover for observing Jeremy. I must memorize his looks, his mannerisms, his way of talking, enough so that I can fool March. Not that anyone would suspect me of shapeshifting, but questions about health and sanity can arise if I act out of character when transformed.

I have a few minutes of surreptitious spying until the couch sags from the weight of another body. Esme grins at me with fire-engine red lips when I turn.

"Hello, Merry. What are you writing?"

"A few notes about my day. I'm a university instructor, and I like to write down any good insights my students had." It's rare that a student has an idea that I haven't heard before, but it's a plausible excuse for the notebook. Esme nods with enthusiasm.

"It's great to see someone take pride in their work. Especially educating young minds. Good for you."

Before she can praise me more, I change the topic.

"How are you faring? After being chosen for the

85

ceremony?"

"Oh, lots to prepare." Esme's face glows with zeal. "My life will change completely. I've taken all my money out of the bank and closed accounts—who knows where I'll go next? I want to be prepared. I sold all the furniture, gave notice to the landlord—I'm a free woman. Ready to take on the next stage of my life. I envision plenty of travel."

"Is that wise? To give up all your possessions, cut all ties?" My heart sinks to my stomach when I look at Esme's eyes, gleaming with fanaticism. She won't be dissuaded, but I must try. "The vagabond life isn't all it's cracked up to be. Are you truly sure that this spirit connection is what you want?"

"Absolutely. Think of what I can do, where I can go. The world will open to me, in ways I can hardly imagine from this limited body. I am ready."

Esme gazes into the distance, seeing her vision of the future while a smile plays on her lips. She can't understand objections in her current state. More and more, I understand that March has created less of an organization than a cult, and they worship the spirit world.

"It was nice chatting with you." I stand. "But I'm starving. I think I'll grab some pizza."

"You too, Merry. See you around."

I approach the kitchen. Jeremy has finished speaking with his companion, and he reaches for another slice of pizza.

"Which one do you recommend?" I ask him. He looks up in surprise.

"Meat lover's, all the way."

I clap him on the shoulder and take a slice.

"My kind of guy. My name's Merry, by the way."

"Jeremy. Say, aren't you the new guy who went with March to find the grail?" He lowers his voice on the last word, as if saying the cup's name will summon it.

"That's me. How long have you been a member of Potestas?"

"Oh, a few months, maybe. A former girlfriend got me into it, and I have to say, I'm hooked. I was really hoping to be picked for the first wave of volunteers, but maybe it's better to not be the guinea pig. Let someone else work out the bugs, you know?"

"Sounds sensible." And also what March is doing for herself. So far, Jeremy seems a good candidate for what I have in mind. "I'm too new to jump in. So, you've been around for a few months. What do you think about March?"

"A strong leader, a caring person, and a beautiful woman," he rattles off without hesitation. I raise an eyebrow.

"Does she have a husband, partner, anyone?"

Jeremy laughs with a hint of incredulity.

"Keep your voice down. She's here tonight, somewhere. Why, are you interested? You're a bit young for her, aren't you?"

"No, not for myself. I just wanted to know more about her. She seems pleasant, but not always approachable. Intimidating, I suppose."

"Oh, she's great, give her a chance. I don't know if I'd ask her out, but only because of her position. I wouldn't want to ruin my membership with Potestas if things didn't work out."

"Fair enough." I bite my pizza in thought. "Good to get the lay of the land. What's the timeline for the ceremony, have you heard?"

"I think they might have found the last piece, but I'm not sure. If they have, then it's only a matter of days. Keep an eye on your email for the call. I know I've pushed back all important meetings for the next week just in case." He wipes his hands on a napkin and tosses it into the garbage can. "I'd better push off. Nice to meet you, Merry. See you at the ceremony."

Not if I can help it. I nod at Jeremy and he makes his way to the exit. I give him five minutes and slowly chew my pizza. When I'm certain he won't return, I follow him out of the door.

In the kitchen of the dark cupcake shop, I tuck myself behind a large refrigerator and grab my lauvan. I studied Jeremy thoroughly while we talked, so I'm confident I can replicate his look. It takes me a few minutes of pulling and knotting, and a few checks in the mirror of the employee bathroom, until Jeremy Barnum stares back at me from the reflection. I smile, and Jeremy's white teeth gleam at me. I take a deep breath, adjust my loosened tie, and walk back into headquarters.

There are paper plates next to the half-eaten pizzas, and I put two slices and a napkin on a plate and walk toward March's office. I hope she's there, and not busy with amulets or checking past lives. I knock lightly on the office door.

"Come in," March replies, and I turn the doorknob and step into the room, closing the door behind me.

March glances up from her computer when I enter, and she gives me a warm smile.

"Jeremy. How nice to see you."

"I thought you might be hungry." I place the plate on her desk. "It was going fast, and I wouldn't want you to go without."

"That's very kind," she says. "Please, sit for a minute." She closes her computer's lid and sighs before plucking a slice off the plate and taking a bite. "I am hungry. Too much to do, I forget to look after myself."

"That's no good." I lean forward. "When's the last time you went out for a drink, just for fun? You're at Potestas all the time."

She tilts her head and studies me with a hint of a smile on

88

her face.

"Why, what are you suggesting?"

"Can I buy you a drink? Give you a chance to let your hair down?"

Her eyes rake my face. I make it as open and guileless as I can. Finally, she nods.

"I'd like that. Thank you, Jeremy."

We stand, and I hold the door open for her. When we pass through the common room, the people gathered there greet March with smiles and waves. All eyes face in our direction, and more than a few glance at me with curiosity. March responds with composure, saying hello to those closest and greeting them by name. It's disconcerting how much they truly adore her.

Outside, a cool breeze trickles between buildings from the ocean, and the sky is shot with pink and orange from the setting sun. March pulls her sweater closer around her torso.

"Let's go to the Brewhouse." I point a few stores down, where light pours out from a brightly lit pub. "It's close, and they have a good wine selection."

Once inside, March perches on a stool along the window's bar table. I collect a bottle of wine from the bar—a nice vintage from Italy, not expensive enough to give away my in-depth knowledge of wines, something Jeremy likely doesn't have—and join her. She is well-versed in pleasant chit-chat, and conversation flows easily along light topics. Eventually, I turn the conversation to my reason for this escapade.

"What's your take on palm reading?" I say after a sip of my wine. March purses her lips.

"As with any of the spiritual arts, it takes the right practitioner, the right invocations, the right amulet, or the right practice. And forecasting the future is often fraught with pitfalls. There are so many ways it can go, how can you be sure that you are interpreting the path that will be, or that by illuminating that path, you aren't influencing your steps so that you will not walk that path after all? It's a difficult art, to be sure."

"Well, I don't know if I'm the right practitioner, and I have no amulet, but I have been researching palm reading in the library. It fascinates me, that the future could be spelled out in the palm of your hand." I hold up my hand in illustration, then lower it. "I wonder, could I practice on you? Would you mind?"

March laughs and holds out her hand, palm up. The charms on her bracelet jingle against each other. The key dangles on the back side of her hand, closest to the ground. Bingo.

"Of course. Please, tell me what you see. Unless it's bad news, of course." She winks at me. "I don't want to hear any bad news tonight. I haven't had enough wine for that."

I reach out with both hands to cup her palm. My left hand holds her hand steady, while my right takes a piece of modeling clay from under my sleeve and then hovers under my left. I pretend to peer at the lines of March's palm while my fingers massage the clay into a thick disk.

"Apparently, there are two schools of thought about what direction to read the heart line," I say. "I've been going with index to pinkie, if that works for you."

March smiles indulgently.

"Let's see what you can tell me."

"Okay, I'll start with the heart line. It begins in the middle, so you fall in love easily." I look up and wink. March laughs. "Good to know. It's also straight, so you have a good handle on your emotions. I can see that. Hmm, but the line is also broken—you've experienced emotional trauma."

Time for the impression. I look up at March, and she meets my eyes. Quickly, I press the clay into the key then peel it away and tuck it back into my sleeve.

"Very good," March says. Her lauvan are minorly ruffled. Perhaps I've guessed correctly? "What about the head line?"

"The head line is straight, long, and deep, so your thinking is clear and focused, and you're realistic. But all those crosses through the line, that shows that you've made momentous decisions. No surprise there, I guess." I laugh and release her hand. "But I'm not very good at it, so it's probably all nonsense. You'd be better to stick with the horoscope than trust my palm reading."

I take a swig of wine, and when I look at March again, she gazes at me with narrowed eyes. It's a calculating look.

"The Jeremy I know wouldn't brush off his findings like that. He is much more intent on his spirit education." She stares at me for a moment longer. "You're not really Jeremy Barnum, are you?"

My eyes widen involuntarily, although I try to hide it. March nods with satisfaction at catching me out.

"I would ask who you are, but I imagine the whole point of your disguise is to hide that fact. You'd better run along. And know this: the next time you enter headquarters, we will have a way to detect imposters. You won't be able to pull this trick again." She stands. "Goodbye, whoever you are."

March sweeps away, leaving me speechless. How had she known? More to the point, how had she guessed that shapeshifting was possible, and that I was doing it? What does she know?

I shake my head to clear it and drop some bills on the bar, then walk around the block a few times to make sure no one follows me. In a nearby alley, I release my lauvan to transform back into myself, then beat a hasty retreat to my car.

March's guess about my transformation shook me, but my mission was still successful. I carefully peel the clay off the

91

skin of my wrist and smile grimly. I'll make the key tonight. Tomorrow, the grail will be mine.

CHAPTER XIII

Dreaming

Axel Gustafsson Oxenstierna af Södermöre, the Lord High Chancellor for Queen Christina of Sweden, ushers me through the doorway and down a long corridor lined with multi-paned windows that allow the early morning sun to dribble through onto the waxed wooden floorboards. Polished sconces between each window are unlit at this hour.

"Thank you for coming, Dr. Bourdelot," he says in a firm voice. His once blond hair and beard are liberally streaked with white, but his sumptuous clothes sit well on his frame despite his age. "The queen has been poorly for months. The court physician can make no improvements and is at a loss."

"I imagine bloodletting is his most common treatment?" I say with derision. "Have no fear. If Queen Christina can be healed, I will be the one to do it. Assuming you can keep your end of our bargain."

Axel coughs.

"I will do my best. The queen is very fond of the newfound treasure, and it won't be easy."

I stop and glare at him. He fidgets.

"Yes, of course, the ring will be yours. As soon as the queen shows substantial improvement."

"Good. The ring is precious to me." Word had reached me in Paris that some hapless Swedish farmer had dug up a box of precious stones and a beautiful, unusual jade ring. It was quickly confiscated by the Swedish crown, and now resides in their treasury. It was a mystery how a treasure like that had wound up buried in a field, a mystery to everyone except me.

"How so?" says Axel. "It looks ancient."

"I recognized it as a family heirloom. I have no interest in the jewels, it's the ring that has value to my family." It was my eighth wife Khutulun's, the ring I gave her on our wedding day. She thought it an odd Western idea compared to Mongol custom, but was enamored, nonetheless. On her deathbed, she begged me to hide it at the ends of the earth, hidden forever as a testament to our eternal love. How could I refuse her dying wish? I traveled to the wilds of northern Europe and buried it in the forest. I couldn't have known it would be cleared for farmland. I need to recover the ring to hide it away once more.

"Well, whatever your reason, I will fulfill your request if you heal the queen. You have my word. She is our sovereign leader, as well as a dear friend of mine."

His mossy green lauvan show no signs of subterfuge. He clearly cares for the young queen. Axel has been advisor to the Swedish royalty since her father Gustavus Adolphus was in power. He must have watched her grow from child to adolescent queen to confident ruler.

"You were right to accept my offer," I say when we approach an ornately carved door.

"I hope so," he says and knocks.

A maid opens the door. Hot, stale air and scent of woodsmoke waft past us, and I wrinkle my nose. Nothing about the air brings health to my mind. The room is dim, with thick curtains closed against the pale northern sun. Three maids dither in various employments, and a man—presumably the court physician, Grégoire François Du Rietz—stands over the bed. Under the sheets lies a woman who, although I cannot describe her as attractive, nevertheless draws my eye from an obvious strength of character. Her large eyes pierce me through. Her shoulders are crooked, and her light chestnut hair is a tangled mess over a face drawn from suffering.

"Your grace," Axel says. "I am pleased to introduce you to the doctor Pierre Michon Bourdelot, the esteemed physician

94

from Paris. With your permission, he will examine you."

"Yes, of course." Christina's voice is weary but firm. "You are most welcome, Dr. Bourdelot. I am in your capable hands. Please show me that your reputation is not unfounded."

I bow low.

"It is my pleasure to be here, your grace. Do I have your authority to take control of your path to better health?"

She waves her acquiescence.

"You do."

"Everyone out," I say at once. "I must examine my patient without distraction."

With nervous looks at their mistress, the three maids curtsey and retreat. The doctor looks immovable.

"You as well, doctor."

"Surely you will need my account of her grace's health?"

"I prefer to make my own assessments."

"For God's sake," Christina curses. "Leave the man to his work. There are plenty of others in need of your services. I am not one of them today."

The doctor's gaze darkens, but after the queen's outburst, there is little he can do. He sweeps from the room without another word. When his footsteps fade from hearing, and Axel has closed the door behind himself, Christina speaks.

"You lack tact, Dr. Bourdelot. My physician will run to my mother and try to turn the court against you." She closes her eyes and sighs.

"Does that displease you?"

"It is your choice, you are the one who must navigate those waters. I am too weary to care overmuch. And tact has never been my specialty, so I am not one to point fingers. But tell me, doctor, what is wrong with me?"

"May I remove the covers?" I need to see her lauvan clearly. While her nightgown poses no problem, the abundance

95

of blankets obscures her burgundy strands.

"If you must." She throws them off herself and lies stretched out fully. She gives me a mocking smile. "Gaze upon the magnificence of Sweden's ruling queen."

She still has spirit, despite her illness. I can observe her body for signs of sickness, such as knotted lauvan. Her strands tell the tale of general malaise and poor habits—she doesn't receive nearly the amount of rest and food she needs, strange in a monarch—but there is a larger problem. Directly above her lower abdomen floats a snarled mess of threads. My latest mentor, the one who taught me the basics of modern medicine, helped me understand what is inside the body, and what is likely the cause of each knotted untidiness I see. It's not strictly necessary, but it's interesting to properly diagnose a condition. I suspect Christina suffers from inflammation of the female organs. Luckily, that is something I can fix.

"My methods are unorthodox," I say at last. "There will be no bloodletting, for one. I will need to do something strange, which will likely last for an hour. There should be little or no pain. I ask you to trust me."

Christina slowly nods.

"You are welcome to try anything that will make me feel better." She reaches for a book on her nightstand. "I will read while you work."

The title proclaims it to be by the Roman author Petronius. I shake my head and remove it from her grasp.

"Absolutely not. You are overworked, overtaxed, and underfed. You must rest your mind as well as your body. No reading for the next few weeks, especially tomes of significance."

"No reading?" Christina's eyes are wide, and her strands suggest the imminent assertion of her status.

"Perhaps, if you are a good girl, I will find you some

suitable reading material in a few days."

She stares at me past her unkempt hair with a blank expression for a long moment. Then she lets out a weak laugh.

"You have nerve, I will grant you that. Fine, no books. But this treatment had best deliver as promised, or by God, you will wish it had."

"It will," I assure her. She leans back with her eyes closed and waves at me to continue. I put one knee on the bed for leverage and begin the slow process of unknotting.

By the time I have smoothed all the strands over Christina's abdomen, the steady breaths of sleep escape her lips. She is still pale, but with the pale of tiredness instead of illness. I sit on a nearby chair and relax after my tedious exertion. My work as a doctor entails a lot of lauvan untangling. I expect I will choose a different profession next time.

After a half hour of repose, Christina opens her eyes. I clap my hands, and she looks startled.

"Good morning, your grace." I stand and walk to the windows. With a swift motion, I yank the curtains open to expose the room to the watery northern sun. "We must have no more dark, stale heat. Clean, fresh air is the best medicine for you now."

Christina blinks at the sudden light. I stride to the door and fling it open. Two of the maids linger in the corridor.

"Your mistress needs a bath, and a hearty meal," I say loudly. They stare at me in confusion, and I clap my hands once more. "Right now, if you will!"

They scurry to fetch food and hot water. I turn to Christina, who watches me warily.

"Rest, cleanliness, and plenty of food will bring back your health in no time. You are too young to be so careworn. You must take some amusement when you can. Your friend, Ebba Sparre, she must be missing you, no?"

Christina's mouth twitches at my mention of her close companion. By Axel's account, they are more than simply friends. I hide my smile as I pull a small book out of my pocket.

"This is the only reading you are permitted for now."

Christina opens the book without enthusiasm.

"Sonnets? I am sometimes entertained by—oh!" She skims the poetry in earnest. She chuckles and I smile.

"To warm the blood. As your doctor, I must insist."

"These are hardly proper," she says as she turns the page to read more.

"Don't be concerned, you don't have to read them with me. Perhaps Ebba will lend a willing ear. Ah," I say as some maids enter with trays and towels. "I will leave you to your ablutions and meal."

"This is far too much," she protests when a maid places the tray before her. "The diet of an ascetic cleanses the body and sharpens the mind."

"And how has that treated your body thus far?" I ask. She flushes in anger and indignation. "As for your mind, by all accounts it is already very sharp. A few weeks of meat won't dullen it substantially."

"We shall see," she says and waves me over. "Come, sit with me while I eat. You may monitor my meat consumption, to ensure it is adequate." She smiles at me with a look that reminds me that this woman has been successfully ruling a country for years. She is built of steel.

"Of course, your grace." I let her take a few bites, then casually mention the real reason I am here, in the guise of small talk. "Even in Paris, the news reached us of the treasure found in a farmer's field. Tell me, is it as glorious as the rumors proclaim?"

"It could hardly be less," she says with true animation lighting her eyes. "It's a small chest, carved with horses in a strange fashion, but the jewels within! Quite magnificent. The crowning glory is a ring, nestled in the center of all the riches. A beautiful green stone, which my advisors tell me is known as jade. It's a splendid piece of jewelry, and I'm quite attached to it already. I have plans to take the setting and place it on a thicker gold band set with rubies to counterpoint the green of the jade."

"It sounds splendid," I murmur. I must bring the queen back to health, and soon. If I don't take the ring before she dismantles it, I will have failed Khutulun. Some would say it doesn't matter, she is long dead and beyond caring. But I have so little to keep—I can at least keep my promises.

"The ring, as promised," Axel whispers. He passes me a small leather pouch. I glance inside. The ring is nestled in a silk cloth, almost as beautiful as the hand it once adorned. I slip the pouch into my pocket.

"You have worked miracles for the queen's health," he says. "Are you certain I can't convince you to stay? You may name your price. The queen would agree."

I laugh.

"The queen's mother would most assuredly not agree. I would have an uphill battle ingratiating myself with Maria Elenore and her courtiers, if I wished. No, Paris calls me back. Farewell, Axel. You have kept your bargain and proven yourself a fine friend."

Axel grips my hand. Our lauvan twist together, to my surprise.

"You are welcome here at any time," he says with feeling. I nod slowly.

"I will remember."

Shaking wakes me from my dreams. Is there someone in my bed? No, it must be an earthquake. Before my befuddled brain can push my body into action, the tremor stops. It is a long time after that my heart ceases to pound.

CHAPTER XIV

Time is of the essence, but I don't want to move too quickly. Breaking and entering is an art, one I am well-versed in. It is Saturday, so I take a leisurely breakfast and mark a few papers. After lunch, I dial Alejandro's number.

"It's time," I say when he answers. "I have the key. Afternoon is the best time to break in—less likely to have someone at home. Are you in for today?"

"I'll be at your place in fifteen minutes." Alejandro's voice is flat and subdued, a far cry from his usual pep. I expected far more enthusiasm, perhaps some excited questioning about how I took the key, but he hangs up immediately.

When Alejandro arrives, his drooping lauvan and long face match his voice.

"What happened to you?" I say without preamble. A quick examination of the lauvan that fan out from his center hint at the source of Alejandro's angst. "Woman troubles?"

"How did you guess?" Alejandro's voice is uncharacteristically belligerent.

"The lauvan that connect you to Jen are snarled and tangled," I say calmly. "What happened?"

I motion for Alejandro to come inside. He steps with more force than usual and kicks off his shoes as if they have offended him.

"My uncle died yesterday."

"I'm sorry to hear that."

"Thank you!" Alejandro gestures at me as if I've proven a point. "That's what a friend says. I was very close to my uncle, it was a big shock." He pauses to collect himself. "I went to Jen's straight after I heard. I guess I was hoping for kindness or sympathy."

I frown. Alejandro implies that he received neither, but that doesn't sound like Jen. He continues in a bitter tone.

"But instead, she says something like, *everyone's life is short unless you're immortal like Merry, you have to take what you can get, here's hoping your uncle didn't waste his life.*" Alejandro stares at me with an expression that invites incredulity. "Can you believe it? So callous and cold. We had some angry words, then I left. And good riddance."

Alejandro's lauvan spasm when he says the last words, and I know that under his outrage, he feels the loss of Jen keenly. I carefully choose my next words.

"Was that exactly what Jen said, or are you paraphrasing?"

"Close enough," he says. "She got her point across."

"Did she perhaps say something like this: *that's terrible news, Alejandro. I'm so sorry. Life is cruel when it's too short, isn't it? I wish we could all be immortal like Merry. Carpe diem, seize the day, right? Life is too precious to waste. I hope your uncle had a beautiful, full life in the short time he had.*"

"No, she didn't say that," he snaps.

"I'm sure her words were different. But do you think that was what she might have been trying to say?"

Alejandro stares at me for several long moments. Then, his body deflates and his lauvan sag. He puts his face in his hands.

"Oh, no. What have I done?" He looks back at me with horror. "The things I said. How could I do that?" He whips his phone out and dials Jen's number. Ringing leads to voicemail, and Alejandro leaves an anguished apology, followed by a pleading text.

"Now that we've dealt with that," I say briskly. "Let's go to March's house."

Alejandro looks at me with hollow eyes.

"I should go find Jen."

"Leave her to cool down. You've said your piece over the

phone. Give her some space until tomorrow." I pat him on the back. "And what better way to distract yourself than with some burglary?"

Alejandro peers at my phone one last time then up at the house number on a wrought-iron gate that cuts across a driveway between impenetrable cedar hedges.

"This is it. Assuming Jen texted you the right address." Alejandro's lauvan twitch when he says Jen's name aloud.

"Looks right. Anyone able to afford a place on Marine Drive in this market has multiple full bank accounts and is on Christmas party invites with their financial planner. March will be here."

I pull over in front of the neighbor's house. Cars drive past while I consider our options. Alejandro cranes his neck to examine the hedge.

"How are we going to get in? The gate has a key pad, and that hedge is thick."

"Can't go under, can't go through…" I say, then glance at Alejandro. "Shall we go over?"

He stares at me for a moment until understanding blossoms on his face.

"Fly over? Oh, yes."

"All right, here's the plan. We transform and fly to the top of that fir tree." I point beside us. "We watch for activity for a few minutes. Once I have the lay of the land, we will fly to the safest place to transform back into ourselves. Understand?"

"Yes." Alejandro's voice holds repressed excitement. "I'm ready."

The prospect of a flight has cheered up Alejandro, as I

suspected it would. Hopefully, it will make him forget about Jen for long enough to keep his mind on the task.

We exit the car and I walk around to the passenger's side. There are plenty of cars zooming by, with many disinterested eyes gazing at us. Someone will notice when we transform into birds.

"Come on." I gesture to the gap between March's cedar hedge and the towering laurel bush of next door. "In here, where no one can see."

"Why don't we just push through the hedge?" Alejandro slides between branches then grimaces. "There's a fence in here."

"Over we go. Hold still." I reach for Alejandro's lauvan and he stops moving with a patient expression, although his strands twitch with excitement over his upcoming flight.

I changed him into a golden eagle only a few short weeks ago, and the pattern of knots and twists needed to transform are still fresh on my fingertips. Before long, Alejandro shrinks in a moment and reappears as a ruffled-looking eagle perched unsteadily on the ground. He tilts his head at me and clicks his beak.

"I'm coming, I'm coming." I swiftly grab the necessary lauvan and yank. After a breathless nothing, I arrive into a dazzling world of sound and detail. Every scale on every cedar leaf is crisp and vibrant, and the roar of traffic is nearly overwhelming. I take a moment to orient myself, to become inured to the foreign senses, then I nod my head to Alejandro and shuffle out of the hedge in an ungainly waddle.

When there is enough room, I spread my wings wide, the blue-gray wings of a merlin falcon, and with a mighty effort, lift off from the ground. I circle in ever-increasing loops, up and up, until the boughs of the Douglas fir beckon. My wings angle for landing, and I grip the branch tightly with sharp talons. Alejandro lands heavily beside me and flaps a few times to regain his balance. I survey the scene below.

March's house is a sprawling, Tudor-style mansion on an expansive treed lot hidden from the road by the towering hedge. Dormers peek out from a steep roof, and a covered area built for driving through protects exiting passengers from the rain. There are no cars in the driveway, but that is to be expected with a three-car garage. I strain my falcon ears to hear past the traffic noise. Although one neighbor is conversing loudly, and another is having their house vacuumed, no sounds emerge from March's house. It doesn't mean there isn't someone quietly reading a book inside, but I don't have definite proof that the house is currently occupied.

That's good enough for me. I turn to look at Alejandro. His gaze is fixed on a spot on the ground and I follow his line of sight. There is a mouse sniffing under a dry leaf in a flower bed, its tiny whiskers twitching clearly in my enhanced vision.

I forgot to make sure Alejandro wasn't hungry before we transformed. He's in mourning and angry about Jen, so he likely didn't make breakfast his top priority. Just as he opens his wings to swoop down from our branch and strike the unsuspecting mammal below, I reach out with my sharp beak and nip him hard on the wing. He squawks indignantly, and the mouse scuttles out of view.

We had better transform, and soon. It's too difficult to fight the impulses of a hungry bird. I open my own wings and glide to a large rhododendron to the left of a side door. Before my talons touch the ground, I release my lauvan and land on steady feet as a human. Grace is the reward for years of practice. Alejandro lands awkwardly on the ground and I press a few knots in his lauvan between my fingers to release them. He reappears in his usual form, sitting on the ground with rumpled hair and a dazed expression. He rubs his arm and frowns at me.

"Did you have to bite so hard?" he whispers. I nod.

"Trust me, you don't want to eat a mouse for lunch. The aftertaste is terrible."

Alejandro looks a little green and accepts my hand to pull himself up. We survey the closed door for a moment.

"How do we get in?" he says quietly.

"I could pick the locks, either manually or with lauvan manipulation. We could break a window and climb through that way. I could scale the wall and see if any windows on the top floor are open." I reach up above the doorframe and pull out a key. "Or we could let ourselves in with the spare key."

"How did you know that was there?" Alejandro looks impressed.

"People are predictable. When you've lived as long as I have, common habits are easy to spot."

The key fits in and slides the deadbolt over with a soft clunk. I hold my hand out for Alejandro to wait, and I open the door.

A spacious coat room is lined with carefully hung coats, rubber boots of various sizes, and a stand of folded umbrellas. The door to the rest of the house is closed, so I beckon Alejandro forward. He tiptoes in and shuts the door behind him with a quiet click.

"Take off your shoes," I whisper. "It's quieter that way. Just in case."

"I thought there was nobody here?" Alejandro gulps and removes his shoes. I stash both pairs behind a pair of black rubber boots.

"I'm fairly certain, but you never know." I shrug and grin. "Let's go."

Alejandro looks like he wants to protest but simply shakes his head and follows me. I open the door and peer out. There is no sound, so I fling the door wide and pad onto the carpet runner in the hallway. Beautiful honey-colored wood floors gleam softly below mahogany wainscoting and ornate picture frames housing serene watercolors. Two chairs reside in the unused space beside the staircase, and they look identical to ones I have sat in during Queen Victoria's reign.

"Where would the safe be?" Alejandro breathes in my ear.

"Let's try the bedrooms."

The carpet runner leads us upstairs, past a grandfather clock on the landing and potted plants on a windowsill. The first door is a bathroom, but the second is a luxurious master suite, with a four-poster bed and pink and gold furnishings. The walk-in closet, however, is devoid of safes, even after I check behind clothes and open drawers.

"Now where?" says Alejandro. He must be feeling bolder now, because he speaks at a normal volume while running his fingers along the nightstand to check for hidden latches.

"An office, then basement. After that, we'll have to rip up floorboards." I say it in jest, but Alejandro looks at the carpet with an appraising eye.

Downstairs, a door off the hallway reveals a study lined with bookshelves over burgundy walls. A sturdy oak desk accompanies a padded office chair and two expensive-looking upholstered wingbacks. Alejandro runs his fingers along each shelf, but I shake my head.

"Check the desk drawer, if you like, but I don't see any evidence of the safe in here."

"What do you mean?"

"There will be some of March's free-floating lauvan swirling around the area. She put the grail in recently, and it is too important to her for her to be calm about it. She'll have shed some strands for certain."

Alejandro looks crestfallen, then he brightens.

"But the basement might have it."

"Then we had best look there."

In the downstairs kitchen, we pass a vast expanse of dazzlingly white counter to find a well-stocked pantry. Inside, hidden behind a discreet door next to an upright freezer, is the entrance to the basement. Surprisingly, it is unfinished. The raw boards of the stairs lead to the bare cement of the foundation. There is nothing here, nothing except a furnace and...

"Look, Merlo. There it is." Alejandro runs to the safe, a sturdy metal box too large and heavy to lift, and drops to his knees. He looks up at me. "Where is the key?"

I draw it out of my pocket then peer at the safe more closely. It has a keypad, with no keyhole in sight.

"Where does the key go?" I say slowly. Alejandro gapes at me, stares at the safe, then frantically searches every side of the black box.

My brain whirrs, trying to make sense of this mystery. Did August lie about her sister's key? If so, she was a very good liar, as she convinced me with body language and lauvan alike. March must have told August that the key opened the safe. But why? I hold the key before my eyes. It is tiny, truly a charm on a bracelet rather than a proper key. But on the shank, there is a roughness that I hadn't noticed before. I squint to see better.

Engraved on the metal, only faintly discernable in the copy I created, is a series of four numbers. Bingo.

My fingers tap the code onto the keypad and the safe clicks open with an accompanying buzz. Alejandro pops his head over the back of the safe, where he examines the footings.

"How did you do it?"

"Through my immense wisdom and superior intellect," I say. When he rolls his eyes, I laugh. "The numbers were carved on the key."

"Tricky." Alejandro shuffles to the front of the safe. "Let's see the famous grail again."

The door swings open on well-oiled hinges. The only item inside is the grail. Its enameled bowl sits directly on the floor of the safe but is barely visible under a thick layer of multicolored lauvan. The metal gleams between the strands in the dim light.

"I remembered it as being bigger," Alejandro says in a contemplative tone. "More impressive."

"That's often the way. Legends elevate reality to epic proportions. Reality can rarely keep up."

"Let's take it and go," he says with a glance behind us.

"Yes, we've been lucky thus far. Perhaps we shouldn't tempt fate."

I reach in to pick up the grail. Before my fingers touch it, a boiling mass of silvery-brown earth lauvan erupts from inside the cup and pushes my hands back. Intense pain enflames my skin and I stifle a yelp with difficulty. At the sight of my palms rubbed raw as if grated along rough granite, Alejandro blanches.

"Now what?" he says.

"I was half-expecting that." I catch a glimmer of silver inside the cup. It must be another amulet. "March was anticipating my attempt to retrieve the grail, so she has it charmed against me. That's why I brought you along."

"Me?" Alejandro glances at my hands again then nods with resolution. "Okay, let me try."

"Good man." I pat him gingerly on the back and move out of the way. "I can heal any wounds you might sustain."

He takes a deep breath then pushes his hands toward the grail. Closer and closer he draws, until both hands cup the bowl of the grail between them. He looks at me with triumph.

"Good," I say. "Now take it out."

Alejandro's fingers tighten, and he attempts to pull his arms out of the safe. He frowns, and his biceps strain. The grail doesn't budge.

"It's not coming," he says. "Why not?"

I bend my head closer to the safe. So thin I can barely see them are dozens of earth lauvan, crisscrossing through the multicolored strands and holding the grail firmly to the ground. I look on the outside of the safe, and similar threads anchor the safe in place. Neither the grail nor the safe are going anywhere without March's permission.

I heave a sigh.

"It's stuck," I say. Alejandro's shoulders slump in disappointment, then he stiffens.

"Did you hear that?"

CHAPTER XV

A click of the front door being unbolted freezes me. We were too slow. What is March doing home at this hour? Doesn't she have businesses to oversee or evil organizations to run?

I curse under my breath and think through our options. The only way into the basement is through the door in the pantry. Our shoes are in the coat room, and although we could leave without them, there is a convenient and hidden exit door in that room. It depends where March goes.

"What are we going to do?" Alejandro breathes in my ear. His lauvan dance with agitation.

"Listen for where she goes, first. If she goes upstairs, we'll make a dash for the exit. If worst comes to worst, I can transform us into mice, and we can scuttle out like that."

Alejandro visibly relaxes.

"Assuming she doesn't have a cat," I add. "And that I can remember how. It's been a while."

His lauvan stiffen again, but he creeps to the stairs without further speech. I follow him, and we listen for clues to March's whereabouts.

Soon, it's clear where she has decided to go, and she's not alone. Anna's soft voice floats through the door as she and March settle into chairs at the kitchen table. My fists tighten. How long will we have to camp out here? Now even my mouse plan won't work. They would notice the door opening from their vantage point and would certainly not leave mice to roam freely. My mouse trick worked much better in the past, when rodents were commonplace in houses.

I sit on the third stair from the top. We might as well get comfortable, since we'll be here a while. Perhaps March will discuss sensitive information with Anna, and we can learn something of interest to make this trip worthwhile. Alejandro follows suit on the fourth tread, and we listen closely.

"I love this tea, March," Anna says. A teacup clinks on a saucer. "Where do you get it?"

"It's a special blend. I'll give you some when you leave," says March. A chair scrapes over the floor, and March sighs. "Oh, it's good to sit for a moment."

"Busy times, for sure. Linda tried to weasel out of meeting duty yesterday, I had to give her a talk about priorities," says Anna. "Honestly, as if everyone doesn't have enough to do."

"Oh, I didn't tell you," says March. There's a pause while she swallows tea. "Jeremy Barnum asked me out for a drink last night at headquarters."

"What?" Anna gasps then chuckles. "You could do worse. He's very put-together, and good-looking, too. Always easy to talk to, that one. What did you do?"

"I went. Why not? It's not every day that a man asks me out on a date, not anymore. You're still young and beautiful, but one day you'll understand how invisible an older woman gets."

"You're still beautiful," Anna says in an admonishing tone. March laughs.

"For my age, maybe. In any event, we went for drinks. As you say, he is quite pleasant to speak with, and that evening was even more so than usual. Quite a charmer." Alejandro glances at me with raised eyebrows, and I grin. "So much so that I started to wonder. And here's where the story becomes strange."

"How so?"

"I finally realized that I wasn't speaking to Jeremy Barnum at all. Someone had taken Jeremy's looks and was masquerading as him."

"What? Do you know for sure?"

"When I confronted him about it, he didn't deny the charge. And when I saw Jeremy the next day at headquarters, he had no recollection of meeting me the night before."

Anna whistles.

"Do you have any idea who he was, or what he wanted?"

"I don't know what he wanted." March sounds pensive. "But I have a shrewd idea of who it might have been. Fiona has been helping me uncover my past lives, and lately I've been making incredible progress. Ever since I had that episode on the boat."

"Dreams of your past lives?" Anna sounds eager.

"Yes, that's right. Have you been having your own?"

"Yes, ever since I touched it. And I think I also know who was pretending to be Jeremy Barnum."

There is silence from the kitchen. Are they smiling smugly at each other? My forehead is damp. What do they know? What did Anna touch?

"There's not much he can do at the moment," March says in a return to her usual brisk tone. "How are preparations for the ceremony progressing?"

"We're ready. The van is loaded, and all participating members will be on site tomorrow. The moon will be new for the ceremony, of course, and the low king tide is perfect. It can't go any lower than it will tomorrow. I sent the sacrifice an invitation for the 'inaugural meeting of the Vancouver Mountaineering Club,' and she attended at lunchtime." Anna laughs. "Too bad she's the only member, and she won't be one for long."

"Now, now," says March in a reproving voice. "No need to be callous about it. She is a regrettable sacrifice for a larger cause. We should honor her for that." There is a pause, then March says, "You're not letting your feelings override the mission, are you? You have confirmed that she has a strong aura?"

"I might have checked her because of who she was with, but Arnold confirmed," says Anna with a hint of sulkiness. "She's the one we need."

"But it was a happy coincidence that she is beloved by our mutual friend," March says. "I understand your impetus, especially given my recent dreams, but don't concern yourself about him. You are worthy to be loved by someone far better. You had a fling with Merry, leave it at that."

My heart stops and my mind races back over the conversation, to the implications. What are they saying?

"I wouldn't take him back now," says Anna with defiance. "You're right, I can do better. Unfortunately for Minnie Dilleck, she won't have a chance to do better herself."

CHAPTER XVI

My ears ring and blood pumps through them, agonizingly loud. Minnie. Minnie is the sacrifice. She will be killed to further the plans of these tea-drinking, gossiping sociopaths. My fists clench and I half-rise.

Alejandro puts a heavy hand on my shoulder. His terrified face is close to mine.

"No," he mouths. "Not yet."

I try to rise again, but Alejandro is stronger than he looks. We tussle silently for a moment, then I desist. Attacking March and Anna now wouldn't necessarily stop the ceremony. Potestas members are too fanatical, too hellbent on their mission. While the loss of their leader would shock and sadden them, Minnie would still be in danger.

And I am under no delusion that March would give up any information under duress, nor that she and Anna are not protected by spirits. They could incapacitate me, perhaps even kill me, and Minnie would have no one to save her.

Anna gets up to leave, and dishes clatter in the sink.

"I'll walk you to your car," says March. "I want to check the supplies in your trunk."

"Will you bring the grail with you?" asks Anna.

"Yes, when I come."

Footsteps tap through the hall, then the front door opens and closes. Alejandro rises and pulls at my arm.

"Come on, Merlo," he whispers in a panic. "Let's go!"

I rip my arm out of Alejandro's grasp and run to the grail in its place on the floor. There is only one thought in my mind: take the grail before March can use it in her merciless quest to gain power, a quest that will take Minnie's life. It's only lauvan holding it down, after all. They can be broken.

I reach out and grasp the nearest brown strands that anchor the cup to the floor, and yank. A few of them snap, but the rest hold firm. A roaring, grumbling noise fills my ears, and the ground shivers.

"Merlo!" Alejandro's panicked voice cuts through the sound. "What are you doing?"

"Taking the grail." I rip again. More strands break, and the floor jolts disconcertingly. A picture upstairs falls off the wall and lands with a shattering sound of glass on hardwood.

I've only broken a scant quarter of the earth threads. What will happen if I snap them all? Alejandro must be thinking along the same lines.

"If you keep doing this, the house will fall down," he whispers urgently, then he grabs my arm again "Come on, let's go before March catches us."

I shake my head, but he's right. It's too dangerous. There must be another way to stop March. I stumble after Alejandro up the stairs and toward the coat room, slip into my shoes, and fall out of the door. My hands shake with fear and anger at Alejandro's lauvan, but I manage to knot the correct strands. I pull at my own, and we flap heavily up and over the hedge. I speak once we have transformed back into our human selves.

"We have to warn Minnie." My voice is rough with fear for her. "Did Anna say they had already taken her? Surely not. Let me call, get her to go to a safe spot."

I whip my phone out of my pocket and dial Minnie's number with a shaking finger. The phone rings. After the fourth tone, the voicemail comes on.

"Minnie, it's Merry. Call me. It's important."

I hang up to call her office and try to ignore Alejandro's worried look.

"Is Dr. Dilleck in?" I ask the receptionist when she answers the phone.

"I'm sorry, she's away sick today. Would you like to schedule an appointment?"

I hang up without bothering to answer. The shaking has spread to my shoulders now.

"To her house. Now." I leap into the car and pull into traffic before Alejandro has fully swung his door shut.

If Jen thought I drove fast before, it's nothing to the tricks I pull out now. Minnie's life is at stake, and I must warn her, to protect her. Even if it wasn't my fault, not entirely, still, I brought her to the wrong place at the wrong time. The thought of Minnie's life cut short far before her time sickens me. My fingers grip the steering wheel with such force that I have a hard time making the next turn. My tires squeal and cars honk behind us.

"Maybe I should drive," says Alejandro, looking pale.

"No time to stop. And anyway, we're almost there."

I screech to a halt outside Minnie's apartment and double-park. Annoyed horns blare behind me, but I jump out of the car without looking and race to the front door. The buzzer yields no better results than the phone. Alejandro joins me when I run around the side of the building.

"Where are you going?"

"Minnie's apartment is on the second floor. I can climb up and look in through the windows."

A ground floor patio furnishes me with a chair, and with the extra height I can reach the railings of Minnie's small balcony. I swing myself up, long-disused muscles straining with the almost-forgotten motion. Alejandro whistles behind me.

"Were you once a gymnast?" he asks.

"I joined a circus for a while," I reply, my focus on Minnie's sliding glass door. We're far enough up that the latch has a few lauvan attached to it, and it's a matter of moments for me to unlock the door. "Hold on. I'll be right back."

117

The living room, decorated with large abstract paintings and an overstuffed couch, holds no sign of Minnie. The kitchen is similarly empty, as is the bedroom and bathroom. A faint waft of citrus drifts past my nose and I squeeze my eyes shut tight. Minnie's scent is painful when she's not here.

Nothing is amiss, and there are no signs of an attack or forced entry. Minnie left of her own accord. But where?

I won't learn anything else from this empty apartment, but I unlock the front door just in case. I vault over the side of the railing and land in a controlled roll beside Alejandro. He looks only mildly startled.

"She's not there." My breath is coming much faster than my activity warranted. My eyes travel to my center, where strands of all colors branch out from my body to join with all those to whom I'm closest. Alejandro's forest-green threads span the short distance between us, intertwined with my chocolate brown ones. But Minnie's navy-blue threads shoot straight down, into the ground. It's unlikely there is a secret cavern under her apartment building, and there is no subway here. That must mean...

"The spirits are masking her lauvan connection to me," I say, my voice barely a gasp. "The earth spirits. I don't know how to find her."

Leaves rustle in a bush nearby, although there is no wind, and gravel underfoot jiggles and trembles as my strands flare out and disrupt objects around me. Alejandro looks around at the vibrations, then he grips my shoulders.

"We'll find her, Merlo." He gives me a small shake. "Keep it together. We'll get the group over, compare notes, and solve this. Minnie is not lost yet."

I stare into Alejandro's brown eyes, wide with concern, and nod. He squeezes my shoulders and releases them.

"Why don't you call Jen and I'll drive?" he says with an

outstretched hand. "I'm too young for a heart attack."

I smile weakly and place my keys in his hand.

"I hope you've driven shift before."

"Grandfather taught me."

"Oh great," I say with a grimace. "Braulio never had much in the way of driving skills. I'll say goodbye to the car now."

Alejandro laughs and leads the way to the car. It's garnering filthy looks from other vehicles as they edge around it. I ignore everyone and slide into the passenger seat with my phone. I hope Jen is free—I need her ideas and level head. Alejandro ducks apologetically and starts the car.

"How can I live for so long and still be surprised like this?" I say with weariness.

"Whoa, that reminds me of a dream I had last night." Alejandro glances at me with a furrowed brow. "You were in it. Actually, you are in a lot of my dreams lately."

"Oh?" I say without much interest. Jen hasn't written back yet, and I don't even have driving to distract me from the gnawing sense of loss and fear that Minnie's absence has created in my gut. "I thought your tastes ran toward the female persuasion."

Alejandro huffs.

"Not like that. No, I've been dreaming of you in the past, or what my mind imagines you'd be like back then. I don't know why it started now—I've known your secret for years—but it's been every night for the past week."

My mind turns over this information.

"Describe one of these dreams," I say slowly.

"They're a bit hazy, but this one was definitely in the past—swords and all that—and we were sitting around a campfire. Someone was trying to make me eat a rat. Then there was a prisoner who was spying on us, and we had to change our plans."

That is an accurate description of one of my memories, too accurate to be guesswork. Minnie dreams of me, too, but I chalked that up to our therapy sessions. Why is Alejandro dreaming, too?

"And there was another one that same night, except you weren't in it. It felt like the others, though. I was in a hall with a big fire, and a dark-haired young woman in a long dress dropped a pottery bowl. I remember that it was glazed red and black, very distinctive. She was really upset. Random, right?"

I wasn't there, but Alejandro just described something that I know happened in exactly that fashion. Arthur's sister Morgan had dropped a serving dish that had been a highly prized gift from a neighboring lord, and she had been sweeping up the shards by the time I had entered the room. Uther had shouted for ages when he found out, and Morgan had come to me for comfort that night, despite the danger of Uther's proximity. How can he know these things? Whose memories is he channeling?

"I have no idea what is happening," I say. "But Minnie was dreaming my memories, too, just like you seem to be. Although, it doesn't sound like you're seeing my memories. I think you're seeing Arthur's."

Alejandro glances at me, his eyes uncertain.

"How? And why?"

"For that, I have no conjecture." I lean my head against the backrest and contemplate. I stiffen. "When was the first dream?"

Alejandro thinks for a moment.

"Last Friday," he says. "The day you got back from the boat trip."

"The day you touched the grail." I stare at Alejandro. "The day you had that strange reaction."

"You think it gave me some memories? I thought you said

120

it wasn't King Arthur's at all."

"It wasn't. But that doesn't mean it doesn't have some other powers. You certainly reacted strangely, and so did March. I wonder what March is remembering now." I recall her conversation with Anna on the phone after the incident. "She knows something now or thinks she does. What did the grail do?"

Alejandro shakes his head in puzzlement and turns into the parking lot of my building.

"I don't know, but we're here. Let's find Minnie first, then we can figure out what my dreams mean."

I snap back into my present worries.

"Agreed."

In my apartment, I start to pace. The walls are too constrictive, when all I want to do is fly away to where Minnie is. But I can't do that until I know where she is. I need to think of a plan to find her, but my mind only buzzes with unanswered questions and intangible fears. Alejandro watches me for a moment with worry in his eyes, then the door opens.

"Merry! What happened?" Jen races toward me. With a murmured excuse, Alejandro sidles to the door and closes it behind him. Jen doesn't spare him a glance, instead throwing her arms around me. I cling to her for a moment, then push her away to talk.

"They took Minnie. They're going to kill her to complete the ceremony. I don't know where she is, nor how to find her." The panic threatens to overwhelm me again, so I beat it down.

Jen doesn't say anything in return, but her expression speaks volumes. I collapse on the couch like a marionette whose strings have been cut and bury my face in my hands. She sits down beside me and places a warm hand on my shoulder.

"We'll figure this out. Okay? Minnie is not going anywhere. We'll get her back."

I grimace.

"I've been around long enough to know promises like that are some of the hardest to keep."

Jen sighs, then squares her shoulders in determination.

"It doesn't mean we don't even try." She grabs my satchel that sits nearby and rifles through it until she extracts a pen and some loose paper. "Here. Write down every place that you know Minnie goes to. And anything else: phone number, address, full name. We will follow every lead." She stands. "I'll get you something to eat while you think. You might need to transform later, and we don't want you distracted."

I smile weakly at her.

"You remembered."

She pats my shoulder again then points at the paper.

"Get to work."

I scrawl Minnie's name and information on the paper, then her work address. I pause. What do I know about her, truly? Not a lot, certainly not enough to exhaustively search for her. She likes being on the ocean, so she might have a membership at the sailing club. I write that down, then throw the pen on the table in frustration. How can I look for her with no information?

Perhaps I am approaching this wrong. I'm certain Potestas has her, not that she has wandered off to go sailing. I need to focus on every lead I have for March and her people. I grab the pen once more and feverishly write down everything I can think of, the addresses of March's and Anna's houses and of headquarters, anything at all. It's a pitifully small list. My face heats as my blood boils. March. Anna. Potestas. Their hunger for power has led to this. They plan murder for their egotistical gain. My breath comes faster. I pound my fist on the table once, hard. Jen pops her head around the corner.

"What's wrong?" she asks.

"Wrong?" I try to control myself, but it's an impossible task. I rise. "This is all wrong. When I find March, I will end her. And Anna, too. And every one of those psychos in Potestas, every single one that even attempts to stand in my way. They have all made their destiny, and I will deliver."

The paper with my notes flies off the table and swirls in the air from the action of my distraught strands. Jen's eyes follow it with apprehension, then flicker back to my face.

"Merry, please don't talk like that. We will find Minnie, and make sure March and the rest are reported to the authorities so they can answer for their actions. Just—calm down, okay? We won't find her unless you keep a cool head."

Jen's words break through my haze of anger. The paper flutters to the floor. Jen picks it up and holds it tight.

"I can't promise that everything will be okay in the end, but I promise I will do absolutely everything I can to find Minnie. Okay?"

I nod mutely then sit on the couch and pass a shaking hand over my eyes. Jen sits gingerly beside me.

The couch jolts and shakes, and Jen squeezes my arm.

"I thought you were calmed down," she hisses. I shake my head.

"That's not me." We wait for the shuddering to stop. My heartbeat takes longer. "The spirits are waking up and preparing for their big debut."

Jen says nothing and merely squeezes my arm again. A few moments pass.

"Take my mind off things until Alejandro gets back with

reinforcements," I say. "What happened between you two, anyway? Your side of the story."

Jen's lauvan bristle at the memory, although she attempts to keep her voice unconcerned.

"Alejandro completely overreacted when I tried to comfort him about his uncle dying. Things between us were amazing, but then he blows up in my face? I don't need that kind of drama."

I nod without comment. Jen sneaks a sideways glance at my face.

"I'm dating Cecil again," she says quietly. I suppress a groan. Jen's golden threads are taut at her revelation. "I think maybe I made a mistake leaving him. I think. It's not amazing, but he doesn't misconstrue my words, so that's something." She sighs and leans back into the couch. "We'll see."

The front door clicks open, and Alejandro enters, followed by Wayne and Liam.

"Good, you're all here," says Jen. "Are you up to speed?"

She avoids naming Alejandro or looking at him. Alejandro looks pained but attempts to mask his emotion.

"I was waiting until we were all together," he says then clears his throat. "Here's the short version: Merry's—friend—Minnie Dilleck has been captured by Potestas. They plan to kill her to fuel their ceremony to bring the spirits to Earth. We need to find her before they do."

I can't sit still anymore and resume pacing. Laid out like that, it sounds so simple, yet impossible. My knuckles crack when I clench them.

Jen holds up the page of notes that I scrawled minutes ago.

"These are Merry's ideas of where to look, and other information about Minnie that might lead us in the right direction." She hands the paper to Alejandro, being careful to not let their hands touch. Alejandro holds the paper out to read it.

"I have names of Potestas members, too," I say with a start of remembrance. "On my phone, pictures from March's office. I'll send them to you right now."

"This is good, Merlo," says Alejandro. "I think we should split up and tackle each lead separately. Who knows how much time we have?" He looks at me with guilt. "All I meant is that we'll be more efficient. Okay, Wayne, you go to Minnie's apartment and turn it upside down for clues. I'll go to Anna's house and see what I find."

"Minnie's front door is open," I add. "And don't forget Anna and the others are likely protected by spirits. Tread with care."

"Noted. Liam, look up the people from Potestas that Merry knows—Esme, Jeremy Barnum, Ben—and find out where they live. Merry—"

"I'm going to back to March's house to get the grail." I say. "I don't care if the house falls down. Failing that, I'll be at headquarters."

My face must reflect my grim determination, because Jen speaks up.

"Don't forget that the members of Potestas are just people, people who may be misguided. Be careful, okay?"

"They deserve everything I give them. They are all complicit, all accessories to first degree murder, and if they get in my way, I will take them down." I speak with a flat finality, and Jen blanches. Then her face flushes with anger.

"Stop it. Join the twenty-first century. We will catch these people and they can be tried in court by the authorities. It's not your place to see justice done. At least pretend to have some humanity."

I am silenced by this. Part of me courses with anger and determination to wreak havoc in the lives of Potestas members, but the other half wonders at myself. Have I lived too long, that human decency and fairness is fading away for me?

"Whatever you planned for me, Alejandro," says Jen. "You'll have to reassign it. I'm going with Merry to keep an eye on him."

Alejandro nods, and the rest are silent.

CHAPTER XVII

"We don't have time to wait around," I say at last into the quiet. "Call me if you find anything."

I sweep out of the room toward the front door. Jen hurries after me but wisely says nothing. She follows me to the car. When I squeal out of the parking garage, she clenches her seat.

"Slow down, Merry," she says in a strained voice. "We can't help Minnie if we're in the hospital."

I grit my teeth. We have no time for Jen's squeamishness about my driving. I wish she hadn't come with me—I could be a lot quicker without her. I breathe deeply, but it does nothing to calm me.

Instead, I push my thoughts toward strategy. When Alejandro and I stole into March's house this afternoon, I changed us into birds to fly over in stealth. I could do that again, I suppose, although Jen has never transformed before and I don't know how she would react in bird-form.

I shake my head. This isn't the time for subterfuge. I don't care if March knows I'm there. In fact, I almost want her to know, so that I can show her what happens to those who threaten me and mine. I have had it with Potestas and their power plays. I want them gone, every last one.

Jen rubs her nose beside me, and I am brought back to her comments in my apartment. Is that why she has been strange around me lately? Does she feel that I have lost my humanity, that perhaps I didn't have any to begin with? Does she worry that because I am from a far-gone era, that I have nothing in common with modern folk?

I sigh, then steel myself. Perhaps not every member of Potestas needs to pay, but March is certainly due for a reckoning. And until I have Minnie safely in my arms, mercy is not in my vocabulary.

Our drive through the darkening streets is silent. When the car purrs to a stop in front of March's property, Jen looks at me.

"What's the plan? How are we going to sneak in?"

"We're not." I unbuckle my seatbelt and get out of the car. She follows. "We're storming the gates. I am retrieving that grail, one way or another."

"What? What if March is here, with a protective spirit?" Jen runs after me as I stride toward the gate between the hedges.

"Then she'll find out exactly who she's dealing with, won't she?"

I run my hands over the wrought-iron gate. My fingers pull lauvan from the iron that is suspended in mid-air by supports, and the removal of threads creates fractures in the iron. Once there is enough, I grab the metal with both hands and wrench it toward me.

With a shrieking squeal, the metal bends and snaps. The jagged hole created is wide enough for us to clamber through.

"Whoa," Jen breathes. "Okay, I guess we're in."

I take the lead and help Jen through the opening, then pace up the driveway without waiting. The paving stones are solid beneath my feet, and I feel grounded and ready for action.

The house looms up before us, white with dark beams and dormers that appear as if the house is watching us. I take the steps two at a time and pound on the door.

"Do you expect someone to answer?" Jen asks breathlessly behind me.

"It would be simpler than breaking in."

There is no response, so I move to the nearest window, take a potted plant from its perch on the railing, and throw. Jen yelps when the glass shatters.

"Did you really just do that?" She looks around anxiously.

"I've never broken the law before."

"I come from a time when laws were a lot more fluid, and I've seen plenty of them come and go." I use another pot to bash at the glass that clings to the window frame. "If March threatens someone I care about, as far as I'm concerned, she doesn't deserve to sit tight and snug in her home. I'm coming to get what's mine."

I climb in and give a hand to Jen, who gingerly steps over the threshold and crunches on the glass strewn across the hardwood floor.

"Downstairs," I say. "That's where the grail is kept. Come on."

"What if somebody is here?" Jen whispers in my ear.

"Wouldn't they have come running to see what all the noise was about?"

"I wouldn't. I'd be worried about a burglar attacking me. Not all of us have fighting skills."

I shrug.

"Then they'll stay away. Works for me. Priorities, Jen. Let's get the grail and get out of here."

In the kitchen, I swing the basement door open and rattle down the wooden stairs. I pause at the bottom and stare in horrified disbelief.

The safe is open, and the grail is gone.

"No," I say, quietly and then with rising volume. "No, no, no, no!"

"What?" says Jen in a panicked tone.

"It's gone. That murdering, smug, cultish, monster March Feynman took the grail already." My shoulders tighten with anger. "They have everything they need for the ceremony."

My limbs shake with barely controlled rage, and my vision blurs. All I can think about is Minnie, scared and alone, lying on a sacrificial stone while March wields a knife above her body, the grail with its multicolored strands in her other hand. How can I let that happen? How can I stop it?

Through the rush of blood in my ears, I can hear rattling and shattering sounds. My lauvan fling around my face, but I don't care. It's not until I hear a scream and a thud that my vision clears. I whip my head around.

Jen lies at the bottom of the stairs, propped up on one elbow and looking disoriented. My anger seeps out of me like a leaky balloon. Did I push Jen off the steps in my mindless rage?

My heart clenches and I drop to my knees at Jen's side. Her eyes focus on me, and she shrinks back in fear. I close my eyes in remorse.

"Jen, I'm so sorry. I was so angry, I lost control. You should never have been hurt." I reach out to touch her shoulder, and she allows me, but her threads remain tense and unsure. "Let me see your head."

She bends forward to expose the back of her head to me. There is a loose knot of lauvan above her hair, but nothing that I can't smooth away. In a matter of moments, her threads are free-flowing once more and she looks up.

I don't meet her eyes. I don't want to know what I'll see there. Does she see me as a monster? Is she right?

"Let's go to Potestas headquarters," I say and hold out my hand to help her up. "That's our next best bet."

Jen is silent behind me. The kitchen is empty when we enter, but footsteps sound in the hall. I creep to the door to look.

A man in a polo shirt with an insignia on it sees me and shouts. I recognize the shirt—he's one of March's security guards.

"Stop right there," he shouts.

I have no intention of surrendering to March's security team. I glance around the kitchen for ammunition. Jen has flattened herself against the wall and stares at me with wide eyes.

"Now what?" she whispers.

"Now this." I grab three kitchen knives from a large wooden block on the counter. They're clearly expensive and have a nice heft to them. I weigh one in my right hand as the man approaches. He pulls out a gun.

"Oh, no, you don't," I say. I step to the right and fling the knife at the man. It flies tip over handle and slices into the man's shirt at the shoulder. The tip plants itself in the wall behind him. He freezes and glances between the knife and me.

I don't wait for his reaction and simply throw another knife with an accuracy born of centuries of practice. It embeds itself in the other sleeve's shoulder. The man drops the gun and it skitters away on the floor. I pace toward him and he pales.

"What are you going to do?" he chokes out.

"Where is March Feynman?" I ask, my face inches from his. His breath smells of stale coffee.

"I don't know," he says. When I make a sudden motion, he babbles, "Honestly, I don't know. My job is to watch the house. Other guys are on bodyguard detail. They don't tell us things we don't need to know. Even if I phoned in, they wouldn't tell me."

I hold the last knife under the man's chin. It scratches against stubble and he lifts his head as far as it will go. His breath comes quickly.

"Stop it." Jen's voice comes loud and stern. "That's enough. He doesn't know anything. Decide if you want a vendetta or a rescue. Because I'm only with you for one of them."

I pause for a moment. The man's eyes search my face, desperately looking for a sign. The knife stays at his chin. Then I jab my hand into his center, swift as a snake, and squeeze hard. His eyes roll back, and he slumps to the floor, tearing his shirt on the knives as he falls.

"What the hell did you do?" Jen rushes to the man's side. I toss the knife on the counter.

"He's only unconscious, you needn't worry. Come on, there's nothing more we can gain by staying here. We need to go to Potestas headquarters."

Jen looks at me with wariness tinged with approval. She stands and straightens her shirt.

"Let's go." She touches my forearm briefly. "Together."

We make our way to the door. On the front porch, my phone rings. Alejandro's voice shouts when I put him on speakerphone.

"Did you find the grail?" he says.

"No luck. Anything on your end?"

"Liam found Esme's and Ben's addresses and phone numbers. He's trying to contact them."

"Good. We're going to headquarters now, see if anyone is around that I can extract information out of." I glance at Jen, who wears a frown at my choice of words. "We're running out of time. Minnie is still alive, but for how long?"

"How do you know?" Jen asks. I look at the threads of midnight blue that are entwined with my own, descending from my center into the porch stairs.

"Her lauvan are still connected to me. If she were dead, they would be gone." I force myself to say the words with detachment, but Jen's sharp glance tells me she isn't fooled.

"That's not all," Alejandro says. "Wayne found the invitation to that mountaineering club in Minnie's apartment, the one that Anna said she sent to draw her to the ceremony. The meeting was at noon today. That must be when she was taken."

I tap my foot in frenzied thought.

132

"The grail," I say at last. "We may not know where Minnie is, but without the grail, Potestas can't complete the ceremony. Jen and I will stop at headquarters. They may have taken it there."

"Okay, Merlo. See you soon. Stay safe, Jen." Alejandro hangs up before we can respond. I shove my phone in my pocket.

"Let's go. With any luck, the grail is still at headquarters."

I screech to a halt in front of Sweet Thing, the cupcake shop that hides Potestas headquarters. Jen is pale and white-knuckled, but she uncharacteristically said nothing while I tore through the dark streets.

Sweet Thing is closed at this late hour, but the door is unlocked as always. I rip the door open and storm inside. I don't care about maintaining secrecy for Potestas, not now. Any aspirations to espionage that I held before this point have evaporated. All I care about is freeing Minnie from the clutches of March and her followers.

I push behind the counter and yank the "plumbing" door open. Jen allows the door to slam shut behind us.

The common area is empty. It's the first time I've seen it thus, and my heart sinks into my stomach at the sight. We're too late. Is everyone already preparing Minnie for the sacrifice? I should have raced here immediately, intercepted March. Now she is far ahead of me, and Minnie is in more danger than ever before.

"Damn it!" I mash my fist into my palm. "They're all gone."

"Check the rooms before we go," says Jen. "Just quickly."

I race to March's office before Jen finishes her sentence and burst through the door. No one is there. The central meeting room is the same. But down in the hall, the door to the amulet acquisition room is partly ajar. I point to it and motion Jen to stay back. Depending on who is in there, I might be able to pretend I am still a loyal Potestas member copto gain information without force.

I peek my head into the room. The shelves are not as full as they were the last time I was in here, and my gut tightens. More Potestas members must have spirit amulets, which means that our rescue of Minnie will be even more difficult. There is only one person in the room.

"It's Arnold, right?" I say into the quiet. Arnold looks up at my voice, then he relaxes when he recognizes me. He pauses his packing of amulets into a backpack.

"Merry, hi. What are you doing here so late? If you're volunteering at the ceremony, it's not until tomorrow morning. I suggest you get some sleep."

"I was just leaving." My voice is rough with anger and fear, and I try to modulate it without much success. "I saw your door open and thought I'd see who was still here."

Arnold's lauvan buzz with excitement, and he doesn't notice my odd behavior.

"I had to grab a few extra amulets, just in case. March said we had enough, but it's better to be safe than sorry." He rubs his hands together. "Do you want to see the barrier I created to contain the sacrifice? I gave the full version to March to take to the ceremony, but my little prototype is here."

He's clearly itching to show someone his genius. My hands clench at the mention of a sacrifice, but I try to answer as calmly as I can. I need to leave but knowing about this barrier may mean the difference between saving Minnie and watching her die.

Arnold doesn't wait for my response. He pulls four rings off a nearby shelf and spaces them evenly in a small circle on the table. Each ring glows with different elemental lauvan—orange for fire, silver for air, blue for water, and brown for earth—and when Arnold hums in a high-pitched tone and passes his hands over the circle, the threads entwine up and around each other to form a dome of glistening strands. My mouth opens.

"What is that?" I whisper.

"Can you see it?" Arnold asks. He glances at me with curiosity. "That's some power you have there." He chuckles with glee and grabs a small wooden box from the shelf. "It doesn't look like much yet, not to me, but wait until you see what it does. We'll have a much bigger one at the ceremony, and the sacrifice will sit in the middle. The spell can only work within the barrier, but there's a bonus." Arnold opens the box and shakes out a shiny black beetle into his palm. "No one can go through the barrier once it's activated. I'm not sure exactly what happens, but they won't be right after. They might even die. So that's a great side benefit—no one will be able to prevent the ceremony from occurring, not without harming themselves. It's a difficult thing we're doing, and I fully understand if someone gets cold feet, but hard decisions have to be made for the good of the many."

Arnold places the beetle on the table and nudges it in the right direction. It scuttles toward the rings then veers away, as if it can sense the dome of strands before it. Arnold herds it toward the dome with his hands, and the insect slowly crosses through the barrier.

Halfway through, it pauses. Its legs begin to twitch. A jolt passes over the black carapace, and the beetle is ejected from the dome. It lies on its back, shuddering spasmodically. Its lauvan convulse, then float away from the beetle and disappear into transparency. The body lies still.

Even if we reach Minnie in time, the barrier will prevent us from rescuing her. My blood pumps loudly in my ears. All I can see is the motionless beetle. Arnold says something, but I'm not listening. All I want to do is end this terrible device and this disgusting farce of a ceremony, starting with Arnold. I step toward him with rage in my heart.

CHAPTER XVIII

Strong fingers squeeze my forearm.

"There you are, Merry," Jen says with warning in her voice. "I was looking for you. Hi, Arnold."

"I'm sorry, I don't remember your name," Arnold says.

"Don't worry about it, I'm pretty new. It's Carly. I just dyed my hair, maybe it's that. See you later."

She drags me from the room. I resist only for a moment. Hurting Arnold would definitely fall under the vendetta category, and I don't have time to waste attacking him, nor do I want to risk losing Jen's help.

Jen opens the door to the next room and shoves me inside. It's the room of reflection, empty but for a few cushions on the floor. I pick one up and throw it across the room, where it bounces off the wall with a soft thump. It does nothing to lessen the storm of emotions raging inside me.

"March has the grail. Minnie's already captured. They're setting up a barrier that strips the lauvan off anyone who crosses it." I choke, thinking of Minnie scared and alone and with no idea of what she's in the middle of. My voice is strangled-sounding. "I can't save her."

I squeeze my eyes shut so I don't have to see Jen's stricken face. Her mouth is open but she's at a loss for words. What is there to say? The woman I love—there's no denying it anymore—will die. They always do, but not this soon. Not before she's had a chance to live. Not before I've had a chance to show her that I love her.

"There must be something we can do," Jen whispers.

My mind races, but it only encounters dead ends. Unless…

"I'm getting the location from Arnold," I say. "He knows where they have Minnie, or where they will take her tomorrow.

He will tell me, one way or another."

I don't wait for Jen's reaction before I turn to the door. I don't want her censure, not over something I know I must do. If it's a choice between Minnie's life or Arnold's, there is no contest.

I burst into the amulet room, and the door crashes against the wall. Arnold looks up with a startled expression from his zipped backpack.

"Tell me," I hiss. I pace toward him with measured steps. My expression must strike fear, for he backs away with dread in his eyes. "Where is the ceremony?"

"If you weren't told, you're not supposed to know," he squeaks out with conviction despite his fear.

Swift as a snake, I wrap my fingers around his neck and force him to press against the wall. His hands grip my wrist uselessly.

"Why?" he gasps. His eyes widen. "You want to stop it."

"Of course, you imbecile. You're going to kill an innocent woman. My woman." I squeeze my fingers tighter in the wave of anger that washes over me. Arnold's hands leave my wrist.

"We've come too far to be stopped by you," he wheezes.

Before I can react, a boiling mass of silvery air lauvan strikes me in the face with the force of a gale. I release my stranglehold on Arnold's neck in a futile effort to protect myself from the hurricane that beats at my watering eyes and whips projectiles into my stomach. I stumble back, blind and winded. Jen's yells dimly pierce the thunderous roar.

Then, silence. I wipe my streaming eyes on my sleeve and take deep, panting breaths.

"Merry, are you okay?" Jen says. I wave in her direction.

"Fine," I gasp. "Where did he go?"

"He escaped. I tried to pepper spray him, but he pushed me over before I could take it out. I guess he has an air spirit connection?"

"It would appear so." I stand upright with a groan. I feel very old, both from the attack and from the weight of my failure. "My last hope is gone."

"It's not over yet." Jen stands with her hands on her hips and glares at me fiercely. "The ceremony isn't until tomorrow. The others are still searching for clues. It's late—let's catch a few hours sleep at your place and then save Minnie at first light."

I stare at Jen's fierce face, then I hang my head in defeat. Centuries of experience, and I can't think my way out of this one. How can I reach Minnie?

I drive to my apartment in a daze. Jen glances at me from time to time but refrains from speech. There's not much to say, after all. My eyes are dry and rough with tiredness, and headlights of oncoming cars make me squint. Damn the frailties of my human body. If I had any leads, any hint of Minnie's whereabouts, my weariness would be forgotten. But with nothing to strive for, my body asserts its needs.

Alejandro and Liam look up with hope when we enter the apartment but wilt when Jen shakes her head.

"No March, no grail, no answers," I say in a hollow voice. "Please tell me you have something."

"We've combed the list of Potestas members you found," Liam says in an apologetic tone. "They either don't respond—presumably they're already at the location—or they know nothing about it."

"We're sure they don't know," Alejandro says in a tired voice when I open my mouth to question their certainty.

"Wayne went and asked a few in person. He got rough, and they still didn't talk."

I stride to the window and look at the city with unseeing eyes and a sinking heart. There are so many places Minnie could be.

"Where would they take her?" I whisper.

Wayne enters the front door.

"I have a cop friend," he says as if continuing a conversation. "Maybe she could look up the phone numbers of the members who aren't answering, figure out where their cell phones are." He rubs his bald head in distraction. "Is that possible?"

"I don't know. And only if your friend doesn't have a strong ethical code," I say.

"I can convince her. She's at work by eight in the morning."

"That's great, Wayne," Alejandro says with forced cheer. "We will be at the station at eight to make sure."

"My geologist friend contacted me again," Wayne says. "These tremors we've been having, they are much more frequent than he expected. Do you think they have anything to do with the ceremony? Spirits, and all that?"

"Yeah." I rub my eyes. "No doubt. This is the big moment for the spirits, being released into our world. They're bound to get frisky. Not to mention the power needed for the ceremony."

"It's all coming together, isn't it?" Jen whispers.

"I'm going to check Anna's house," I say. Four pairs of surprised eyes look at me. "I doubt she's there, but I have to do something." I unlatch the patio door and step out.

"Merry," Jen calls out.

"I won't be long."

On the balcony, my fingers seek out the necessary lauvan. A moment later, my falcon-form thrusts upward with powerful wingbeats into the night sky.

Stars blaze overhead, far brighter with my bird eyes. I catch an updraft and circle higher. When the city is merely dots of light below, I aim my wingbeats toward Anna's house.

I've flown here in darkness before, and my memory does not fail me. Within minutes, I land on soft grass before an imposing older house on a quiet street graced with tall deciduous trees. I release my lauvan and dissolve into my human form with a sigh of relief.

The house is dark, but that is not unexpected at this hour. Curtains on the second floor are closed, so the only way I can make sure Minnie isn't here is by breaking in. I don't wish to alert the neighbors with cracking glass—they are far closer to the house than in March's neighborhood—so I flit to the front door and begin to work on the strands that surround the lock. There aren't many, and it's a matter of moments before the deadbolt slides across.

The hall is dark, and the moonless night sheds no light over the threshold. I leap up the stairs with light feet and swiftly check the rooms for inhabitants. All beds are empty, and the closets as well. I wouldn't put it past Anna to shove Minnie in the back of one.

The rooms downstairs are similarly vacant, and a dank crawlspace yields no Minnie. Outside, I transform once again. It's astounding that I'm able to fly at all with such a heavy heart and lead in my stomach.

I glance at Minnie's dark lauvan that travel from my center to the ground and close my eyes briefly in pain. I must find her tomorrow, whatever it takes.

My balcony is easy to spot, since it is the only one occupied.

141

Jen has pulled out a couple of chairs and sits in one with her feet on the railing and a mug of tea clasped between her palms.

I circle down and transform with perfect timing to land heavily in the empty chair to the sound of Jen's gasp. I slouch and reach for the bottle of beer Jen has thoughtfully left for me on the floor.

"Do people ever get used to that?" she says.

"Eventually." I take a deep pull from the bottle. Effervescence tickles my throat pleasantly, until I remember that Minnie will have no more such pleasurable moments unless Potestas is stopped. The beer turns bitter in my mouth and I don't take another sip.

Jen doesn't speak for a long time, not until I finally do.

"I was with Isabella for forty years," I say at last. "She was the daughter of a butcher. Her favorite color was yellow. She adored sunsets, dogs, and marzipan. When she danced, her eyes would glow with a light to rival the sun. I held her as the spasms of death ravaged her body, from a fever that spread like wildfire that winter." I take another sip of my beer. The bitterness is fitting, after all. I sigh. "How did it come to this? I truly wanted to avoid love and the heartbreak that inevitably follows. How did Minnie sneak her way in?"

"Isn't it better to have loved and lost than to have never loved at all?" Jen says after a sip of her tea.

"Perhaps that applies to some, but I have had more than my share of loving and losing."

We remain in silence for a few minutes, the only sound coming from an occasional car on the road behind my building.

"I don't have much comfort to offer," Jen says finally. "Not beyond the promise that we will do everything we possibly can to find Minnie. But maybe you'd like a distraction?"

"How so?" Not much could distract me now, but I'm content for Jen to try.

"I've been dreaming of you," Jen says with a smirk.

"Not you, too?" I groan, then sit up straight. "Wait, what kind of dreams?"

Jen looks perplexed at my reaction but answers readily.

"They are like something out of history class. It must be from you telling me about your past, and all my questions. Now my brain is fired up and making up all sorts of crazy stuff." She sips her tea with a pensive air. "They're every night, though. For over a week, now."

I sit back and contemplate. First Minnie, then Alejandro, and now Jen dream of my past. Alejandro touched the grail, but what about Jen and Minnie? Am I sloughing off lauvan that carries memories with them?

"Minnie and Alejandro have said something similar," I say slowly. "In all my long years, I've never come across this. I don't know what to say."

"Oh, well, they don't do any harm." She yawns so widely that her jaw cracks. "Some are a bit gory, but nothing I can't handle. I'd like to see them now, in fact. Let's get some sleep so we have energy for our search tomorrow."

"You take the bed," I say. "I'm used to hard surfaces."

CHAPTER XIX

Dreaming

Running. Branches lashing at my naked skin. Rain plasters hair to my forehead. Rain dripping

dropping

dribbling

sizzling   on   my   fevered   flesh.   Dogs howl—wolves—dogs—in my head?

I slip in mud. Sprawl headlong. Mud between fingers, toes, in my ears, hair. The shock stops my mad rush. Why fight the mud?

Oozing under my nails

cool, grounded

part of me

Voices sing, deep grating sounds, no words but I recognize it all the same

hypnotizing

mesmerizing

part of me

Lauvan of the earth wrap around me, tighter than a mother's embrace. This is where I belong. Voices like a lullaby. I close my eyes.

Nimue's pale face. Bloodless. Lifeless. Dead because of me, I who will not die.

I surge from the mud with a squelch. I run. Rain washes my body but cannot wash Nimue's face away. I run to her. I run from her. If I run fast enough, her death face will leave me alone. I can leave the guilt beyond guilt behind.

I run.

CHAPTER XX

I sleep terribly, from a combination of worry over Minnie and restless dreams. I hate dreaming of my period of madness. It is unsettling and always reminds me of the pain of losing Nimue, so quickly on the heels of losing Arthur. I spiraled into a sort of wild lunacy and roamed the forest for years before I could claw my way to normalcy again. By that time, even more of my friends had died.

But the dream had a purpose. I sit bolt upright from my blanket on the floor. The spirits. That's what the voices in my dream must have been, although I didn't know it at the time. Why do I always forget about the spirits? They will know where the ceremony will take place. And after previous encounters, I'm sure I am strong enough to force them to answer. I don't care what it takes. I'm going to contact the spirits. The spirits want to come to this world so badly? They'll have to get through me first.

I rise, careful not to wake Alejandro, Wayne, and Liam sprawled on the couch and floor of my living room, and find my satchel. The amulet that Anna gave me is still there. I don't know if I need it to contact the spirits, but it can't hurt to have a little help.

We are far too high in the apartment, however. I know, instinctually, that I must be on the ground to feel the earth spirits best. That, and there are very few earth lauvan up here. I slide out of the front door without a sound. While I wait for the elevator, a throat clears behind me.

"Going somewhere?"

Jen stands with arms crossed beside me. I nod curtly.

"Getting answers from the earth spirits. They will tell me what I need to know, or there will be consequences."

Jen nods and says nothing else, but when the elevator arrives, she steps on board with me.

Once outside, my shaking fingers pull the wristband from my pocket. Earth lauvan swirl around my hands and gently touch the strands there. I take a deep breath, then close my eyes and send my mind into the strands as I do with a lauvan cable.

To my surprise, presences immediately surround me. Inquisitive prods touch my consciousness, but I don't have time for niceties. With all my will, I visualize grabbing one of the presences and pulling it out of the stream of strands.

Chaos reigns. Presences batter my mind with the force of pelting stones, but I don't let go. The presence I contain rages back and forth, rough as rock and as implacable as a mountain, but I'm stubborn too. One by one, the other presences flee and leave their fellow in my grasp. Did I frighten them? Good.

I open my eyes and pull the presence out with me. I have no idea what will happen, but I have one now and I can't let go, for Minnie's sake. This needs to end.

The strands that entwine around my wristband bubble and grow. My fingers quickly lay the wristband on the ground. A figure emerges from the strands, its shape vaguely humanoid. Its rough features give the impression of fear and annoyance.

"You have ensnared me," it says in a deep, gravelly voice. Jen gasps at the sound. I smile briefly in grim satisfaction.

"Yes. I have questions that must be answered."

"You have been told, everything will be revealed by the successor once the ceremony is complete." The voice sounds slightly petulant. I suppose these spirits aren't used to being bested.

"That's not good enough. You're planning to sacrifice a human to complete the ceremony, and I can't let that happen. She is precious to me."

"You could choose another," it says. "But with the risk of

angering the successor."

"Who is this successor?" I mash my fist into my palm. Again and again I hear the same story. I need answers, and I need results. Minnie is counting on me.

Even though its features lack the true expressions of a face, it still manages to look surprised.

"You truly do not know? I assumed you were disregarding the elemental side of yourself on purpose, not out of ignorance."

"What are you talking about?"

"The successor is one of the fundamental earth elementals. I am but a minor elemental compared to the successor. Earth elemental lives are long compared to the others—fire elementals last for only weeks—but yet we too must be reborn on occasion. The predecessor was old, and when he died, the successor was reborn out of his essence. The balance must always be kept, the same number of elementals always."

"While this is undoubtedly fascinating, what the hell does it have to do with me?"

"I will come to that, but you cannot understand without knowing what comes before. Long before you were born, we elementals moved freely between our plane and your physical world. Some even donned human forms and procreated with humans. But with that procreation came imbalance to the world. We are not meant to create more of ourselves, we are only reborn from the death of another. The fundamental elementals gathered all of us and constrained us to our plane of existence, and destroyed all those creations that remained, to restore the balance.

"The predecessor grew restless and found a way to come to the physical world. There, he formed a human body, and met a human woman. When the child was born, the joining of human and spirit, and in a few years grew into his powers, the other fundamentals knew what had been done. Rather than having his child destroyed, the predecessor agreed to enter a state of stasis, a sort of half-life, in order to restore the balance and allow the child to live. He stayed in that state until his death.

"That child is you. I am surprised you knew nothing of this. You have lived for long enough, surely you would have discovered the truth before now. Your human and elemental sides are closely entwined, but still separate, after all."

The spirit finishes. Jen and I stare at each other. My mind releases my hold on the spirit in my shock, and the brown strands shrink with haste into the wristband.

"I guess that explains a few things," I say in a hoarse voice. "I'm not totally human. That legend about my father being a demon? Looks like it's not far from the truth."

Jen shakes her head, back and forth, expressing her confusion.

"That's insane." She rubs her face. "But what do we do now?"

That's right. Minnie still waits for us. With all the revelations, I didn't force the spirit to release her, or give us the location. But I'm armed with new knowledge.

"We go find Minnie, even if I have to take down every last one of those sorry-excuse-for-a-human Potestas members." I wince at the mention of "human." What am I? "This is not over."

Jen doesn't say anything in reply, only holds the door open for me.

When we enter my apartment, Liam calls out.

"Where have you two been? I got into Esme Rotari's email. Genius, right? And guess what? I know where the ceremony is!"

148

CHAPTER XXI

We're quiet in the car. Jen sits in the passenger seat, clearly unwilling to leave me alone after the spirit's revelations. I drive automatically, with my mind far away, traveling down centuries of questions and seeking and wondering.

I'm not human. Or, at least, not entirely. My father was an elemental, who somehow managed to create a child with my mother. I don't begin to understand how that might work, yet it must have, because here I am. My lauvan float in front of me and the two different types of strands stand out clearly, now that I know what I'm looking at. My own solid, human strands are more substantial than the fine elemental threads, although precisely the same color.

"Merry?" Jen says with hesitation. "Are you okay?"

"No," I answer. "I'm not. My whole understanding of myself and my place in the world has been turned upside-down, and I have no idea how to right it. I don't know what I am. But it doesn't matter. The only thing that matters right now is that Minnie is scared and alone, with would-be murderers surrounding her. We're all that can stand between her and death, and I don't care how many barriers Arnold constructs, nothing will stop me from being by her side."

Jen nods with moist eyes.

"Yeah. Yeah, I get that." She sniffs. "We'll bring her home. We'll figure it out. And you're not alone, Merry. We're all going to be there, doing whatever we can. Alejandro will be there, of course. Wayne, Liam. I told Cecil what was happening, and he insisted on meeting us there."

"Cecil? He's always the surprise." I glance sidelong at Jen. "He and Alejandro must be having a cozy tête-à-tête right now."

Jen flushes but ignores my last comment.

"I think your neighbor Gary came too."

"What? Why?"

"He wanted to help? I don't know, Alejandro just texted me that, I didn't ask further."

I sigh explosively.

"I hope he's up for it. I don't want to have to take care of anybody. I have Minnie to save. You lot will have to take care of yourselves."

"We're not here to be a burden," Jen says with frustration, then her voice softens. "We're only here to help, and we'll stay out of your way when you need us to."

I nod tightly. I hope she's right.

"What do you want to tell the others about—you know, your spirit-ness?"

"I can't see how it's relevant right now. We have more important things to do than sit and chat about my heritage."

"Okay, got it." Jen pauses. "Do you want to talk about it now?"

"I need to think and plan, Jen. A few minutes of peace, please."

The parking lot is half-full when we arrive, but our group is easy to spot. I pull into a nearby space and Jen and I hop out. The stench of low tide hits me in the face like a blade of rotting kelp.

"Are you all sure you want to do this?" I say without preamble. "This may get messy. I can't guarantee anyone's safety, and I can't promise to protect you. My primary goal is to get Minnie out of there."

"We know, Merlo," Alejandro says. "We are here to help. Just lead the way."

I nod, then scan the parking lot. There are two trails down to the shoreline, but only one with copious amounts of lauvan swirling between the barricades. The Potestas members were clearly excited by the upcoming ceremony. One navy-blue strand floats past my face and I swallow hard. My fingers brush against it and I sense Minnie's distress and confusion.

"This way, everyone." I point at the trail. "I'll go first. Alejandro, walk with me."

Alejandro jumps to my side and we lead the line of my friends in a swift hike down a gravel path beside a crumbling cliff of loose rock.

"What is Gary doing here? Did you tell him about me? I don't want him freezing because he can't handle lauvan, spirits, all that."

"He overheard us in the hallway and wanted to help. He's pretty spry for an old guy, I think he'll be fine." Alejandro glances back at Gary, who gamely pushes on with the others, a baseball bat resting on his shoulder. "I told him about your powers, and what Potestas might be able to do, and he was fine with it. He has an open mind."

I scrub my face but keep walking.

"Someone else added to the initiate list. Don't misunderstand, not having to hide from those I care about is liberating, but one day someone won't react positively, and I'll have to leave." I look into his eyes for emphasis. "Please don't forget that."

Alejandro looks contrite.

"I'll remember."

The shoreline is expansive, a far cry from the usual crashing waves against the cliff. Muddy silt sticks to our shoes as we pick our way between decomposing sea stars and heaps of drying seaweed. Tremors occasionally shake the ground beneath our feet, but the ground shivers only enough to convince me that I have mild vertigo. We walk for ten minutes, the gleaming multicolored strands growing more frequent, until we turn a corner around the cliff. Scrubby grasses hang over our heads, and the highway noise drifts down from far above. Someone waits for us beside a large boulder.

"He's here," a shaven-headed man in a blue polo shirt says into his walkie-talkie. "With others. Back-up needed immediately."

"My reputation precedes me," I say lightly. "Then you'll know that I'm going through you, regardless of your back-up. Stand aside."

"I can't do that." The man pulls a handgun out of his holster. "Put your hands—"

I don't let him finish. His nervous neon-green threads spark out from his body in spasms, and I yank at the nearest one. He bends double in pain and his gun drops to the ground. I run forward and kick it away with a spray of muck in its wake.

"That's enough of that," I say. A quick squeeze of his center renders him unconscious, but a yell from behind me makes me whirl around.

Three more polo shirts have emerged from behind the boulder. Wayne grapples with one, Alejandro and Liam take another, and the others run toward the third. Cecil dives for the gun of the guard before he can draw it, and it falls to the silt. Gary punches him in the stomach, and he doubles over, wheezing. Jen hovers with her pepper spray, but when the guard is incapacitated, she runs to Wayne. He and his guard punch each other with fierce blows, but when Wayne breaks away for a moment, Jen sprays the guard's face. He screams.

Alejandro and Liam scuffle with their guard for a few moments more, but the guard is overwhelmed by the numbers and they soon have his arms behind his back. Jen takes a good look at him then gasps.

"Barty? Is that you?"

The guard peers into her face.

"Jennifer Chan? What are you doing here?" His expression is bewildered.

"Was the security company bought by March Feynman?"

"Yes, yes it was. What, who…" He looks around at us. "What are you doing with them?"

"Long story," Jen says. "Do you know what you're protecting today?"

"Information is on a need-to-know basis with Ms. Feynman," he says with a hint of resentment. "We're supposed to stop this man." He points at me. "And anyone else who is with him."

"March is going to kill someone," Jen says. "You're protecting murderers. We're here to stop them."

Barty stares at Jen for a moment with confusion in his eyes. Sucking noises announce the arrival of more guards tromping through the mud.

"I know that's not you," Jen says quickly. "You used to give me candy as a kid. You're better than this. March Feynman is doing terrible things. You don't want that on your conscience."

More guards burst out from behind the boulder with guns drawn.

"Stand down!" Barty yells. "Stand down. There's been a misunderstanding." He looks at Jen with indecision. "We should come with you."

His strands twist with discomfort and uncertainty. I shake my head.

"Thanks for the offer, Barty, but we have it covered. Don't dig yourself in deeper than you need to."

Barty glances between me and Jen, but when Jen nods encouragingly, his lauvan relax.

"Everyone back to the parking lot," he says to the other guards. "This job is over."

"We're on the clock for another two hours," one guard says.

"Look, it's on my head, okay? I'll sort it out with management. Back to the van, now."

Alejandro and Cecil release their guards, and the pepper-sprayed guard is helped to his feet by his fellow, who hauls him up gingerly and tries to avoid the liberal mud smeared across the guard's back. Barty stops in front of Jen.

"I hope you're right about this," he says to her. "I'll be likely demoted, if not fired."

"It was the right thing," Jen says. "An innocent woman's life will be spared." She wraps her arms around him in a swift hug. "Thanks, Barty. And good luck."

"You too." He looks around at us all. "You too."

CHAPTER XXII

Barty and his guards walk up the beach without looking back. I turn the other way and squelch around the boulder. The shoreline continues, jagged and with plenty of places to hide. There's no time to waste in talking or pondering other people's actions and reactions. There's only Minnie, waiting. Waiting to die, waiting to be saved. I walk faster.

The sloughed strands grow ever thicker, until I am nearly wading through them. There are many different colors, and my heart sinks. How many people will I have to move out of my way before I can get to Minnie? I don't care about harming them, not after they aligned themselves with a murder plot, but the more I must mow down, the slower I will be. March only needs Minnie and her volunteers to complete the ceremony, after all.

"Merl—Merry," Jen stumbles on my name. "Sorry. That was weird. Do you know where you're going, still?"

"The trail is thick with lauvan," I say without breaking stride. "It's not difficult to follow."

"Good." Jen looks ahead then gasps. "Who's that?"

A figure leans against a sheer rockface, entirely at her ease. Short, spiky orange hair frames a sharp face with an upturned nose above a smug smile. Her arms are crossed over her chest, and a ring on one finger dances with fiery orange strands. My own mouth sets in a grim line.

"A Potestas member. She's enhanced with a fire spirit. Watch out."

Her smile only widens as we approach. Her face is shaded from arbutus trees that cling tenaciously to the cliff above her. From behind another rock, Ben appears. A cuff of leather wraps around his wrist, barely visible below swirling brown threads. His eyebrows lift.

"Merry. They said you might be coming, but I could hardly believe it. I thought for sure you were on board, after volunteering to get the grail." He rubs his chin. "Is it because you have your own powers, that you don't want the spirit ones? Because I got to tell you, they are pretty amazing. You should probably reconsider."

He and the woman chuckle.

"I would be less concerned about you and your fellow egomaniacs gaining powers if you hadn't kidnapped the woman I love," I growl. "But since you have, I might as well kill two birds with one stone, as it were. Rescue her and get rid of the lot of you."

Jen glances at me but says nothing.

"You should stop," Ben says. "We're too powerful. It's futile to try."

"Tell that to Drew Mordecai," I say. Ben looks discomposed. The woman laughs.

"Let him come. I've been dying to give my spirit free rein. I want to see what happens." She puts a finger on her jawline in question. "But why did you help get the grail if you want to stop the ceremony?" I don't answer, and her face clears in understanding. "You were trying to steal it, weren't you? Gotcha. Too bad March is too clever for you. How did you find us here, anyway?"

I glance at the ground behind them, where the path of strands gleams like a rainbow.

"I have my ways."

Neither of them reacts to this, although the spirit strands on their amulets give a jolt at my words.

Jen and others cluster close to me and I whisper instructions under my breath.

"The woman has a fire spirit and the man has an earth spirit.

Split into pairs and disperse so they can't target all of us at once. I will engage them, the rest of you act as back-up."

Jen grips her pepper spray tightly and nods when I make eye contact. The rest look nervous but prepared. Even Gary has changed from a genial old man to an energized, grizzled soldier. His shoulders are straight, and his gaze is clear.

I turn and pace forward with deliberate steps. Behind me, the sucking noises of feet walking through mud indicate that my instructions are being followed. Ben and the woman straighten and plant their feet firmly. Fire lauvan blossom from the woman's ring and entwine around her arm and neck. With her orange hair, she looks like she is aflame. Earth strands plunge from Ben's cuff down his legs and connect to the ground he stands on.

I take a deep breath. Can I use the new-found knowledge of my heritage to my advantage? I haven't had long enough to fully ponder the extent of its usefulness. I'll have to fight how I normally fight and hope that it will be enough. Perhaps an idea will come to me in the heat of the moment. Necessity is the mother of invention, after all.

My thoughts are interrupted by a trembling in the Earth below my feet. I stumble then look at Ben, whose concentrating face holds a smile of satisfaction. I keep my balance with difficulty and follow his gaze to Liam, who edges sideways with Alejandro, hoping to avoid detection. A great groaning noise emerges from the ground, and pools of water envelop Liam's feet.

"Liam, watch out!" I shout, but my warning comes too late. The Earth yawns beneath him in a slimy hole, and he drops with a yell.

"Liam!" Alejandro falls to his stomach and slides forward to look into the hole, but I have no more attention to spare the two. A crackling sound makes me whirl around.

An arbutus tree that clings to the cliff above me is aflame, its branches lit with an unnaturally quick-spreading fire. The whole thing is lit like a torch, and the sudden heat is intense. A larger crack alerts me to danger, and I leap out of the way of a falling limb. Its blazing length crashes to the beach in an explosion of sparks and burning debris.

Another branch falls. Wayne shouts, and Cecil dives to Gary to pull him out of harm's way. Gary brushes sparks off his clothes with quick motions.

I use the mayhem to take a few steps closer to our two enemies, but the woman laughs.

"Nice try," she says. She raises her arms and fire lauvan dance off them as if she is a human bonfire. Another tree on the cliff whooshes alight, then the first tree groans. Ben stares at its base, and the earth trembles enough to topple the tree. With a screech and a crack, the whole gnarled mass roars down to the ground. Wayne and Gary are directly in its path.

"Move!" I scream. Wayne and Gary's wide eyes track the tree, then they both dive to the side. The tree thunders to the beach and lands with a tremendous crash. The impact shudders the mud beneath my feet.

I turn back to my foes, who both watch me with complacent smiles. They don't notice Jen, who was not idle while the tree fell. She is almost upon them both and holds her pepper spray up with a steady arm. She narrows her eyes in concentration.

Ben tracks my gaze and whirls around. Before Jen can react, he stamps his foot in a petulant manner. If I'd wanted to laugh at the gesture, it would have died in my throat. Quicker than thought, the mud rolls under Jen's feet as if she rides on ocean waves. The pepper spray flies out of her hand and she falls. The silty waves roll her farther and farther away until she is covered in muck and hidden behind new hills in the otherwise flat beachscape.

"Jen!" I yell, but there is no answer. I lift my hands in readiness and start toward the pair again. Before I can reach them, Wayne comes barreling out of nowhere and throws a mean punch to Ben's face, who only just manages to dodge it.

The woman points her arms straight up, and from the overcast sky above shoots a bolt of lightning. I am blinded by an intense light, and my ears are deafened by a tremendous crack that reverberates through my body. My ears ring in the aftermath of the bolt, and when my eyes can see once more, Wayne appears unscathed although clearly shocked. There is a patch of blackened soil beside him.

Ben's face is red with rage.

"You could have hit me, you idiot! Don't pull out the lightning again, you hear?"

I may be rattled, but I have too much experience not to take every advantage that presents itself in a fight. I leap toward the woman, who looks partly chastised and partly indignant.

"You're welcome!" she yells. "You weren't doing so great yourself, you definitely needed a hand."

She doesn't even see me coming. With a snarl, I push her to the mud and bury my fingers in her center. The elemental fire strands immediately surround my own and my skin starts to burn, but I grit my teeth and ignore the pain. One quick squeeze, and the woman relaxes into unconsciousness. Without a human to guide them, the fire strands retreat to the ring.

Wayne doesn't miss the opportunity, either. While I knock out my opponent, he punches and kicks at whatever part of Ben he can. Ben cowers before the onslaught, but before Wayne can take him down, Ben slams his cuff against the ground with a snarl.

Waves of silt mound up under Wayne's feet. He loses his balance, and the waves carry him away. They grow far higher than they did with Jen, so high that they curl at the top, then crash down like a wave on a steep beach. Wayne is covered with mud, choking in it, and by the time the waves subside, he lies facedown, half-buried in the silt.

I run toward Ben, who turns much more quickly than I anticipated. The ground under me gushes water and crevasses form. Ben's spirit is creating another sinkhole, but I'm not unprepared. I push off the unstable ground with all the strength I can muster and soar toward Ben. His expression of surprise is almost comical.

I slam into his body and we roll out of the sinkhole's reach. Ben throws a few wild punches at me, but he is clearly not a practiced fighter and I defend myself easily. I could punch him back, but my focus is on his lauvan. My fingers seek purchase on his center, but the strands there are strangely slippery. The ground continues to tremble from Ben's spirit traveler. I need to subdue the spirit somehow. Ben's flailing aggravates me, and I press my arm into his neck to contain him while my other hand wrestles with unlatching the cuff. Earth strands form a barrier around the cuff, and my fingers can't penetrate. If I can't take it off, what can I do?

My eyes close and I send my mind into the lauvan surrounding me. Every time I try this, it becomes more straightforward. The presence of the earth elemental is there, right there, and with my will I force it away. It doesn't put up much of a fight and flees until no presence touches my mind. When my eyes open, no earth strands cover the cuff.

Ben looks at me with a terrified, incredulous stare.

"What did you do?" he whispers hoarsely. "Where did the spirit traveler go?"

"I told you not to mess with me." While we talk, I debate what to do with Ben. Render him unconscious? Tie him up? "I don't take kindly to anyone harming those I care about. You

160

fall into that camp."

Ben splutters indignantly, but I glance up to find the trail of lauvan. I became turned around during the chaos, and it is our only guide to the ceremony site.

It's nowhere. No gleaming rainbow path stretches over the silt, no matter where I turn my head. My heart pounds almost painfully in my chest. Where is my arrow that points to Minnie? Have the spirits somehow erased it?

I thrust my hand against Ben's neck without warning. His eyes bulge.

"Where is Minnie?" I yell. "Where did you take her? The spirit path I was following is gone."

Ben shakes his head.

"I won't tell you," he forces out. "We will connect. You can't stop us."

I squeeze his throat harder. He makes a choking, glottal sound. His head is half-submerged in the muck and sinking deeper.

"Stop it, Merry!" Jen shouts. She must have crawled back from the silty waves. "You're killing him!"

I don't care. I need to make him talk. He has to understand that his life is on the line, that if he doesn't tell me where to go, I will end it. His eyes are frightened but not yet terrified. I can change that.

My free fingers enter the nest of strands at his center. Slowly, I start to squeeze. Ben's body shudders, then spasms.

"You will tell me," I whisper then squeeze harder. Ben's shaking intensifies. Through the blood pounding in my ears, as if from a great distance, I hear shouting but ignore it. Finally, the expression in Ben's eyes show me what I want to see.

A tight hand around my wrist loosens my grip on Ben's throat, and another relaxes my hold on his lauvan. I let go and stand. Alejandro stares at me with concern. Gary and Cecil are silent, and Jen's nervous eyes look at me through her mud-covered face. They don't know how far I'll go to save Minnie, but they're starting to guess. The unease is palpable. I would worry about how this will affect my relationship with my friends, but right now I have more important issues to handle. I look down at Ben, who gasps and coughs weakly on the ground.

"Well?" I say. "Where is she?"

When Ben collects himself enough to focus his streaming eyes on me, he points down the beach where the rainbow strands used to lie.

"Walk to the next corner." He pauses to cough. "Turn right past the massive boulder. There's a cave behind it that's always covered except for the lowest low tide. You can't miss it."

"Get Liam," I say to Alejandro and point at the sinkhole. "I'll find Wayne."

Alejandro and Cecil shuffle cautiously to the edge of the sinkhole. I run past the new hills of silty sand piled up between us and the distant water.

Wayne lies facedown in the muck. I skid to a halt on my knees beside him and turn his body to face the sky. No air lauvan enter or exit his mouth, and my heart stops. Is his airway full of silt? Carefully, I grasp the strands of the muck in his mouth between my fingers and pull up.

Silt bubbles out from between Wayne's lips and drips down his muddy cheek. Moments pass, and still more emerges. Can I extract it all? Will Wayne breathe again?

A choking cough rasps out of Wayne's mouth, and my shoulders sag in relief. I turn him to the side and he vomits up the rest of the disgusting muck. When he is ready, I help him sit upright.

"Welcome back," I say in a hoarse voice. "I thought you

might have left us."

"I'm tougher than that," he says with a ghost of a chuckle. "Can you give me a little pick-me-up? A lauvan boost? Is that possible?"

"Absolutely," I say. "You'll have to sleep it off later, mind you."

"I can do that."

I twist a few pertinent strands above Wayne's forehead, and his bloodshot eyes change from weary to clear and bright. He stands up with enthusiasm.

"Come on, Merry. We have a damsel in distress to save."

I slap him on the back, relieved more than I can express that he is alive and well, and we rejoin the others. Liam has crawled out of his hole with the others' help, and beyond the ruination of his clothes, looks in good health.

Wayne's right. It's time to continue our mission. I turn in the right direction, but before I take a step, Ben speaks again.

"It doesn't matter what you do. You'll never get through the barrier."

I lunge at him. I have no intention of doing anything beyond startling him, and my goal is achieved. Ben pales and shrinks away. I let out a huff of disgust and spit at his feet.

"If you've led me on the wrong path, I will come and find you again," I say. "And I won't be as merciful."

I don't bother waiting for a response. Minnie waits for me, and this interlude has kept me from her for long enough already. I break into a run and leave Ben and his unconscious companion far behind. The sound of pounding feet tells me the others follow.

CHAPTER XXIII

I don't slow down enough for anyone to catch up to me. I don't need to feel Alejandro's conciliatory pat on my arm or see Jen's reproachful gaze after my treatment of Ben. I do what I must to protect those I care about. I only hope I don't lose their regard for me through my actions.

The beach is clear of lauvan, but Ben's directions were simple. My feet push off the sucking mud with as light of footfalls as I can manage, so eager am I to come to Minnie's side.

At the next corner, I turn right with unhesitating footsteps. The only sounds behind me are footfalls and ragged breathing. I push harder. Minnie is waiting. When my fingers brush the strands that connect us, even though they descend into the earth and give no hint of direction, they still vibrate with confusion and terror.

A lauvan cable emerges from the distant ocean and runs directly through a long, narrow bay to a dark gash in the cliff at its end, beside a truly massive boulder left from the last ice age.

Two figures emerge from the tunnel. One shouts and points at us.

"Watch yourselves," I call back. "We have company."

I feel rather than see the others cluster closer together. I soldier on. The figures from the tunnel haven't acted yet, and I want to put in as much distance as I can before they make their move.

We're three-quarters of the way to the tunnel when the rumbling starts. It finally makes me stop and look up.

The cliffside is falling away, rocks rolling and sliding toward us, soil and gravel kicking up into the sky with the force

164

of the motion.

"Landslide!" I yell. "Everyone run back, as far as you can."

Shrieks and panicked footsteps tell me my instructions are being followed, but I don't join the others. Instead, my fingers feel for the right strands to transform. A moment later, powerful wings thrust my body into the sky. I'm a merlin falcon, one of my favorite forms, and perfect for evading landslides. A quick glance behind reveals the others safely out of the landslide's path, staring ahead with shocked looks but safe. I turn my focus to the guards. With a shriek, I flap toward them. When I'm close enough, I dive.

A diving falcon is no laughing matter. I'm a bullet of feathers, tipped by a beak of ferocious sharpness and backed by talons of the same. While I don't have the speed of a peregrine falcon, I'm fast enough.

The guards yell and dive out of the way, but it's simple for me to adjust my trajectory. At the last moment, I pull out of my dive and point my talons down. They land on one guard's head, and it's short work to gouge out an eye.

He screams and bats at me with clumsy arms, but I dive out of the way and flap above him. A whooshing sound turns my head. What is that?

The other guard must control an air spirit. A huge wave of wind barrels down at me, invisible to all but my eyes. It's a boiling mass of air threads, promising destruction when it arrives.

In a flash, I release my hold on my strands and my body reforms into its human state. I drop to the ground, winded but heavy enough to withstand the hurricane that washes over us. There is a blast of pressure, a howling of winds, then it's gone as quickly as it came.

I don't wait for the guards to recover. Quick as a snake, I throw myself at the uninjured guard, the one who controls the air. His eyes widen in terror and his lauvan, air and human alike, freeze in shock. It's a matter of a moment to thrust my hand in his center and squeeze him into unconsciousness.

The Earth shakes under my feet. Damn, is there another guard? I look up but the guard I thought I had already dealt with glares at me with hatred. One hand covers his injured eye, which bleeds through his fingers and drips down his chin, but the other points to the ground with outstretched fingers. Earth strands pour from a cuff on his wrist into the sand.

There's a tremendous crack, and my head snaps up to look even as I dive out of the way. A moment later, rocks from the tunnel entrance crash on the ground where I was standing. The guard grimaces and points his fingers down again.

Before I can react, Cecil takes a flying leap from behind me and throws himself at the guard, who yells in pain. A pulse of energy flows through the earth lauvan that connect the guard to the ground, and another shower of rocks pummels the two.

"Cecil!" I shout. When the rocks stop falling, I jump to his side. The guard is unconscious, knocked out by his own rockfall. Cecil breathes heavily and looks pale.

"My leg," he forces out. "I think it's broken."

I shift a good-sized boulder off his shin. It lies at a strange angle, and bruises are already forming. I wince.

"Looks like it." I press my lips together and glance at the tunnel, then reach for his leg. Cecil puts a hand out to stop me.

"Come get me later, okay? I know there's not much time. I'm not going to bleed out here, right?" He looks to me for confirmation. I shake my head.

"No, but…" I glance at the tunnel again. Jen skids to a stop beside us with a concerned look on her face. Cecil pushes my shoulder.

"Go. Just come fix me once you're done in there." He lays back on the ground and takes ragged breaths.

"What?" Jen says. "You can't just leave him, Merry."

"There's no time," says Cecil again.

I reach into his center and tweak a few strands, and his face relaxes.

"That should help with the pain. Thanks for coming to my rescue, Cecil."

He smiles with his eyes closed.

"Go get her. Man, whatever you did for the pain is awesome."

I stand and look around. Everyone else has arrived. They look wide-eyed but ready. Jen dithers for a moment, then kisses Cecil's cheek and stands. I wave at the dark tunnel.

"Here we go."

Before we take five steps, I stop everyone.

"There's no point in going in blind." I say. "Let me see what I can sense up ahead."

There are a few confused noises from the group. I ignore them and plunge my hands into the cable that runs along the tunnel's edge, a great pulsing shimmery cord of light as high as my waist. The painful pleasure threatens to overwhelm me, but I grit my teeth and force my mind to travel down the cable's length.

The cable winds along a twisting path, ever up and up. It doesn't take long before a gleaming disturbance of human lauvan appears, two clusters of them, and then a great glowing center where at least six cables intersect, and many more human lauvan clusters wait. The intersection point throbs with a strange energy that I've never seen before. A tremor shakes my feet, and I watch in fascination as the cables pulse outward from the center. I send my conscious back to my body and open my eyes with a gasp.

"There are two guards at the entrance to a central cave, and many more people in the cave itself. Until then, we have clear sailing."

"How…" Wayne starts, then shakes his head. "Never mind."

Jen passes me a flashlight. Everyone else already holds one.

"Good thinking," I say to Jen. She smiles grimly.

"I'm rarely unprepared these days."

We set off into the darkness, illuminated only by our yellow circles of light. The floor is smooth and sandy, and the walls are of jagged rock, with a ceiling higher than I can reach. Everything drips, and the scent of rotting seaweed is pungent. Alejandro catches up to me.

"I felt the barrier where they're keeping Minnie," I tell him. "It's around a center, where lauvan cables cross. It's a place of great power, so it's no wonder March chose to do the ceremony here. The spirits must have guided her to the right spot."

"Did you find anything out about the barrier?" he asks.

"Nothing useful. I'll have to wing it when we get there."

The tunnel floor rises in a steep incline, and the sand is loose underfoot. The tunnel steadily becomes drier as we rise above the high tide line. After a few more minutes, my flashlight beam illuminates a sudden drop. The tunnel opens into a wider cave. My light picks out a few details—hints of rock formations that look like waterfalls, jagged crystals, and endless stalactites and stalagmites—although the beam is too dim for my eyes to pick out anything more than tantalizing glimpses of unearthly beauty. Behind me, gasps echo in the cavern.

"Yes, the cavern is beautiful," I say. "But now we have to climb into it."

I get on my hands and knees and shuffle my feet down until I have a foothold on the cliff. It's no more than a ten-foot drop, and I scale the rough rockface easily. We've climbed far enough up that this cavern would never be submerged. The others follow more slowly, but all manage, even Gary, who is helped by Liam. The only sounds are our breaths, footfalls, and the muffled dripping of water. The air is dank and stale. Jen shivers beside me.

"It's gorgeous and terrifying all at once down here," she says quietly. I rub her arm in reply then carry on through the cavern.

We circle around the stalagmites, but the path is clear before us. The sand shows a trail of footprints that lead to the far end of the cavern. The ceiling is rippled with smoothly carved bowl-shaped hollows, as if giant bubble of lava popped and solidified up there long ago. The tips of stalactites drip from low portions of the ceiling, and our path skirts a veritable sea of matching stalagmites. A quiet waterfall flows out of the side of the cavern wall and runs beside the path, dark and glistening in the light of our flashlights. The water shivers with earth tremors, which are only minutes apart, now.

After we silently traverse the cavern, the path leads us to a narrow tunnel leading up once more. We file in one by one, and I take the lead. The ground is rough, but there is enough height that we don't need to stoop. The occasional sandy patch shows footprints.

The path inclines sharply, and I put out my arm to stop Alejandro. The rest jostle to a stop.

"I think we're almost there," I say. "I remember this slope. Let me check."

Sure enough, when I plunge my hands into the cable, the two human clusters from before are a minute's walk away. I pull my hands out and face the others.

"Quietly, now. See if we can sneak up on them."

At the top of the slope, the tunnel widens until it is as wide as four outstretched armlengths. Large boulders are strewn across the floor. A glow of rainbow light from an unseen source silhouettes two figures who stand with their backs to us.

I point at Wayne and Jen with a finger, illuminated by my flashlight, and indicate that they should sneak to the right. I point Gary, Alejandro, and Liam to the left. The flashlights wink off and a faint rustling indicates they are following orders. I bend down and flit from one boulder to the other, straight up the middle.

When we have moved halfway up the widened tunnel, one guard turns. It's Jeremy Barnum, the man I impersonated to gain access to March's key. He scans the tunnel and must see movement, for he releases a strangled yell. Before he can summon a spirit, Wayne flies out of nowhere and tackles him to the ground. Jen is right behind him, and she ties Jeremy up with rope she must have packed in her backpack. She really was prepared for everything.

The other guard shouts and rushes to Jeremy's aid, but Alejandro leaps out of the shadows toward him. The guard is too quick. Before Alejandro can reach him, brown lauvan boils out of his shirt and into the ground. A split-second later, the roof above Alejandro trembles, then it cracks into a thousand shards of jagged rock and plunges down to bury him.

My heart pounds and my fist clench. No. We are here to save Minnie, but I'll be damned if I lose Alejandro in the process. My lauvan stream outward, shooting straight for Alejandro. It feels like when I've lost control in the past—objects fly around me, pictures rip off walls—but today, I pour my intent into their movement. I want to lose control of them. Only in that sensation can I find the power to bend them to my will. It's a strange juxtaposition that I have no time to dwell on.

All this happens while the rocks still fall. My strands find the lauvan of each tumbling rock and latch on. There is a minor struggle with whatever spirit controls the rockfall, but I brush it away as I would swat a fly. The energy of each shard, the force of their falling, fuels my own movements. My eyes narrow in concentration, and the rocks halt their trajectory. They begin to swirl, slowly at first, but soon they form a maelstrom around Alejandro. When they have enough speed, I send my intent.

Each piece of rock launches itself toward the guard, whose slack-jawed wonderment allows him no time to respond. Within seconds, he is buried under a pile of stones until only one twitching leg remains exposed. Soon, it stills.

Silence reigns. All eyes are on me, but I seek out Jen's first.

"Should I have done something differently?"

Jen shakes her head slowly. Her face is hidden in shadows.

"I don't see what you could have done. You were defending Alejandro. They were going to do the same to him." Her breath hitches, then steadies. "You had to save Alejandro."

I nod. Perhaps I could have knocked the man unconscious, where he would have stood a chance of recovering, but controlling strands the way I just did is new to me. Do I have that finesse yet? I doubt it, and I am not willing to play around while the lives of my friends are on the line.

"Is everyone all right?" I ask and look at Alejandro. He nods, shaken but determined. There is a small chorus of yeses. "Then let's face the music. We're here."

CHAPTER XXIV

The entrance to the tunnel, where the guards were standing, is the top rim of a huge cavern. It's almost as wide as a playing field, and it is shaped like a giant soup bowl. The cable from our tunnel slinks down to join five others at the center of the bowl, where a large dome of multicolored lauvan covers the center. The cables pulse with energy, and the ground shivers with greater and greater intensity. We can see clearly in the heart of this mountain only because Potestas has set up three large spotlights that shine up and create a soft glow that reflects off the cavern's ceiling. At least fifteen people mill about in the bowl, but my eyes are drawn to the still figure kneeling in the center of the multicolored bubble at the intersection of the cables.

Minnie's eyes are wide and there are tear tracks on her face, although she is dry-eyed now. She watches March and Anna, who prepare something near the bubble. My heart squeezes. We're so close, but she's in the barrier. How can I get her out?

Shouts and yells alert me. We've been spotted. I fill with rage and determination. We're getting Minnie out of this. I look to each side and see the same grim resolve on the faces of my friends.

"Ready?" I ask. They nod.

"Let's get the bastards," Wayne says and leaps down the slope with a yell.

I'm right behind him and catch up shortly. A dozen Potestas members stand between us and the barrier. Most look terrified and run behind the dome. Three, however, look smug with the knowledge that they have a weapon that we don't. I glance at each as I run and notice that those three have elemental lauvan swirling around their wrists. Only three? We can get past that.

I hope.

"These three have spirits," I shout to the others. "Green shirt is water, carrot top is fire, and black boots is air."

"Got it!" yells Wayne and sprints with Alejandro close behind toward the red-headed man, who raises his hands in reply. Orange strands coalesce in the air and swirl in front of him. Wayne dives below the forming ball of fire and takes out the man's feet.

I would love to watch more, but there are others who demand my attention. Jen and Gary have teamed up, her with a pepper spray in each hand and him with his baseball bat. Both yell with fury and barely masked terror, but they don't hesitate. Liam follows Jen and Gary to the man in the black boots, so I focus on the woman in the green shirt. She paces toward me with a grim smile. Her outstretched arms glimmer with blue water strands and her own gray ones. They rise to meet a tendril of blue descending from the distant ceiling. I look up. What was once a drip has turned into a gushing torrent, which pools in the air above green shirt's head. She grins wider.

I'm not interested in a bath quite yet. I edge sideways until Wayne and Alejandro and their fiery opponent are directly behind me. Perhaps they would like to cool off.

"What are you waiting for?" I shout. Green shirt scowls.

"Nothing," she says, and makes a throwing motion with her arms.

At the last second, I dive to the side. The jet of icy water barely misses me, and mist wets my face. Carrot top doesn't fare as well. His fireball is doused instantly, and he shoots across the cavern floor to land insensible in a sodden heap. Wayne and Alejandro are drenched from the spray but are otherwise unharmed. Wayne's face is covered with red blisters, but he grins.

"Thanks, Merry!"

It occurs to me that in the chaos, I have grown close to Minnie's cage. I glance at it.

Minnie strains against her lauvan bonds. Her mouth opens and closes soundlessly as if she shouts, but the barrier won't allow sound to pass. She stares at me through the swirl of elemental lauvan. I try to infuse my returning look with hope, but I can't look for long. Green shirt has decided to make another move.

We're close to the barrier now, very close, and when I backhand her, her head swings around rapidly and she stumbles to the glowing lauvan bubble. Horror crosses her face. She staggers, almost rights herself, then falls hard through the barrier.

Her confused eyes widen then roll back until the whites show. Her limbs spasm, and her lauvan twitch at random. Her mouth opens in a silent scream. With a last, savage jolt, she stills. Her blue and gray strands cease their random movements and drift away from the body into transparency. She looks naked and strange without them.

On the far side of the barrier, barely visible through the swirling threads, March and Anna prepare the ceremony. They hold the grail together with their eyes closed, and their lips move in synchronous chanting. They are in their own smaller bubble of protection adjacent to Minnie's larger one. Esme stands behind them, her eyes darting nervously between them, Minnie, and her fallen comrades beyond. Lauvan on the grail swirl with agitation and connect one by one to strands in the cluster of cables that join beside it. There is even one cable that descends straight into the earth below us.

I'm distracted from this disquieting sight by a chorus of voices. My eyes focus on the barrier before me. Dozens of figures emerge from the swirling dome in the shape of humanoid torsos that sway in a breeze not of this world. The

174

voices speak with the grumbling of earth, the ethereal nature of air, the sibilance of water, and the sharpness of fire.

"We want to be released."

"Let us be one of you."

"Don't deny us what you already have."

"The successor is waiting to speak to you."

"Then bring him out!" I shout, fear and exasperation sharpening my voice. More figures bud from the barrier-dome and sway, attached by their legless torsos.

"We cannot," a brown figure growls. "He will only be free once the ceremony is complete. Only then can he tell you everything. Then, you can join him and be one of us. You can have everything you desire."

I pause to gather my thoughts. The spirits wait for my response. I shake my head slowly.

"If Minnie Dilleck survives today, that is all I desire. Nothing you can offer would compare, would be worth the loss of her life." I look into Minnie's eyes, with their mixture of terror and hope. Although she can't hear me, I speak with my eyes locked on hers. "I may not be fully human, but I can use my spirit nature to further my humanity. I can save the woman I love."

March and Anna's chanting grows louder, until they almost shout the words. Their barrier must not be soundproof the way Minnie's is. The strands of the barrier swirl faster and gleam with a pulsing brightness. The torsos of the spirits begin to sink into the fluid dome.

"Pretty words," the earth spirit says before it disappears. "But you are too late. The ceremony is nearly complete. When the earth tremors cease, we will be free."

CHAPTER XXV

Half-formed ideas push to the forefront of my mind, none of them of much value. The spectacle of green shirt's demise in the barrier crosses my mind in full detail. How do I avoid her fate? I wrap my fist in my coat and attempt to push it through the barrier, but the elemental lauvan travel straight through the fabric. The skin of my hand smarts from the contact, then the sensation fades. I pull away my sleeve and look closer.

My own strands have divided themselves neatly in two. My thicker, human strands cringe away from the barrier, rolling themselves up my wrist to escape. The thinner threads, those that I now know are of my spirit nature, pass through the barrier easily. My mind churns. The spirits plan to transfer their lauvan to a human host once the ceremony is complete. Is there any reason I can't do the same with my human strands? The spirits need a ceremony to complete their task, but my physical form can manipulate lauvan without that need. And with my human lauvan safely stripped away, nothing would stop me from entering the barrier and disrupting the ceremony.

"Alejandro!" I shout. He sprints over.

"What do you need, Merlo?" he asks with panting breath.

"Hold still." I comb through my center, attempting to tease out every thicker strand I can feel. Beside me, the barrier releases flashes of electricity that must be visible to Alejandro, because he jumps, and his eyes grow wide. "I need you to hold onto my human lauvan for me. Then I can go through the barrier."

"What?" Alejandro's brow creases in confusion. I forgot that only Jen knows about my big revelation.

"I'll explain later. Just, stay alive, please. For both our

176

sakes."

The ground rumbles below our feet, and the light show from the dome increases in splendor and horror. To Alejandro's credit, he doesn't shift from his position, simply bends his knees to absorb the shaking. Even the Potestas members huddled on the side of the cavern have frowns of fear at the phenomena.

I finally hold a cluster of thick brown strands in my hands. I'm certain that when I pull it away from my body, the rest will slither out and follow the cluster. I take a deep breath—I hope I'm right in my theory—and tug gently away from my body.

My eyes darken. Sound muffles then winks out entirely, leaving only a void of silence. I feel nothing, not the clothes on my body nor the discomfort of my injuries. My senses have disappeared.

Instead, the world exists as if I'm in a lauvan cable. I can sense the strands of everything around me. The barrier looms large, its elemental lauvan fiercely strong. Clusters of other strands bob about the cave, indicating the location of my friends and the Potestas members. Alejandro's lauvan, his life essence, is clear in front of me. Although I can't feel my arms to move them, I concentrate on pushing my cluster of human strands up and closer to Alejandro's. My body must respond, for my cluster drapes over Alejandro's and latches on as if happy to find a body once more.

I am now free of my human lauvan and concentrate on moving toward the barrier. My spirit strands remain in the approximate shape of a human body, so I presume my physical form is walking with me. The elemental strands of the barrier boil angrily at my approach, but I continue. As I pass through, they attack as one.

My lauvan are pushed and battered, but there is no pain—I have little connection with my body in my current form, beyond motion—so the spirits' attack is less effective now. I endure the barrage of sensation for a moment, sensation that is entirely new to me, as it has no connection to the five senses I am used to. I gather my will, my concentration, my desire to get through, and with a mighty force, I push. The spirits soar away from me, their confusion evident in my mind. The last to go are a few stalwart earth spirits, who seem more stubborn than most, but I have their number. I'm part earth spirit too, and I can dig my heels in with the best of them. At the insistence of my pushing, they eventually release their hold and fly away.

My focus is now on Minnie. Her lauvan call me from the center of the dome. I can sense them shivering with fear, and dancing with excitement at my approach. I wish I could interact with her somehow, tell her it will be all right, even simply smile in reassurance, but I don't know how to control my body beyond forcing it forward. It will have to be enough.

Her strands reach out to me, yearning. My own respond willingly. Now, how to take her out of this barrier? Above us, the swirling elementals have reached feverish motions, and every few seconds, all strands shake from earth tremors. Whatever the ceremony entails, it is almost complete. I must remove Minnie before it is too late.

Her human lauvan won't tolerate passing through the barrier. The spirits will attack and destroy her. But what if I could protect her? I will my arms to collect her strands, comb over her body until they are central in a cluster on her front. I am as gentle as possible, but the disruption must affect Minnie, for the cluster drops as if she has collapsed on the ground. I hope I can get her through on my own.

I push my senseless arms to wrap around the space where I estimate her body to be and lift until her cluster is chest height once more. I will myself to move to the edge of the dome. On the way, my spirit strands weave themselves around and over Minnie's cluster. It's the only protection that I can think of. I hope it is enough.

The spirits wait for me at the barrier. Their agitation is palpable. They are already fired up from the near-completion of the ceremony, and now I threaten to take away a key piece at the crucial juncture. They attack with everything they have.

I bend under the onslaught, but it's not only my own survival that I defend. Minnie relies on me, and that thought fuels my rage. I force every scrap of willpower I can muster into my defense. They're strong, too strong, and I waver.

Then I think of Minnie's beautiful eyes gazing into mine, and her declaration.

"I'm not going anywhere."

I push back with everything I have. One by one, the spirits falter and fall away. When the last one whirls away in a flutter of strands, we burst through the other side.

Alejandro's strands are right there, surrounded by my own brown threads. I try to lower Minnie's body carefully to the ground, then reach out to grab my own strands. They slide away from Alejandro as if eager to rejoin their spirit counterparts. I mash them in hastily—they will fall into place on their own—and when my sight and arm dexterity return, I comb Minnie's lauvan back into place.

Sound reappears, shouting that has little meaning to me. As the dimness of my eyes fades, Minnie's supine body appears. She is pale and unmoving and looks so fragile. I tease her strands outward as gently as I can. When they are in place, she still hasn't woken. I stand and survey the cave.

Potestas members press against the wall of the cavern, tied together by their wrists and guarded by Liam. The barrier is gone. Did the spirits leave when their mission had no chance of being completed? Anna is pinned to the ground by Wayne, who wraps duct tape around her ankles while she curses. Gary holds Esme's hands behind her back. She looks angry but resigned.

Jen is in a tug-of-war with March over the grail. March's look of livid concentration is matched by Jen's fierce purpose. They aim kicks at each other, but neither gives an inch.

I start toward them. March looks over at my approach. Her eyes widen. She gives one more attempt at a pull, which Jen counters, then she lets go and turns to run. Jen flies backward with the grail and lands on her bottom with a gasp.

March is gone in a flash, scrambling up the embankment and disappearing into the tunnel. I reach down to pull Jen to her feet.

"We're letting her get away?" she asks. Incredulity raises the pitch of her voice. I shrug.

"What does she have now? No grail, hardly any followers, a loss of trust with the spirits—she's toothless. Let her run."

Jen shakes her head but doesn't comment further. I turn to look at Minnie. To my intense relief, she is sitting up on her own. Alejandro kneels beside her and speaks in a low voice. Whatever he says must be soothing, for Minnie only nods with a dazed expression.

"I'm sorry," I say to Jen. She looks at me with surprise. "For the way I've been acting. Seeking vengeance, not only saving Minnie. Although it looks like I'm only half human, so I suppose it should be no surprise if I don't show much humanity sometimes."

Jen elbows me. The familiar gesture takes me by surprise and reminds me that it has been a while since Jen has acted that way with me.

"Don't be silly," she says. "Isn't love a typically human emotion? Everything you've done has been fueled by that. And you've shown mercy plenty, too, even if you had to be reminded sometimes." I glance at her and she grins. "I'll just have to come to terms with you being multifaceted. I mean, not only are you from a different time, but you're partly from a different plane of existence. But it's like you told me once—deep down, everyone wants the same things. We're not that different, really."

I nod slowly. Jen's words lift a weight off my shoulders that had settled there when she started being afraid of me, and only got heavier when I found out my heritage. I might be different, but I'm not alone.

"I think I'm starting to get it, that's all I'm trying to say," Jen says. She elbows me again. "We're still good friends, right?"

"Always," I say, and put my arm around her shoulders.

I watch Alejandro's ministration of Minnie. He's now joined by Wayne and Gary, who have finished duct-taping their prisoners. Minnie appears bewildered by the attention but relieved that she is surrounded by friendly faces.

My chest feels too small for the emotion trapped inside. Minnie is safe. She will live to see another day, and I want to be there to see it with her, by her side. I hope she can forgive my harsh words from earlier. I can't deny my feelings anymore, and I don't want to. The future will come, there's nothing I can do about that, but I can live for today. Perhaps I will unravel at the end, but some things are worth the risk. I look at Minnie's pale face and hopeful smile and think of the future that might be ours to share.

"Uh, Merlo?" Alejandro calls out. "Did you take back all your lauvan from me? It's just that, well, I think Minnie is a very nice lady, but I'm sure I don't want to do the things I'm thinking about with her."

I leap to Alejandro to a chorus of laughter from the others. My cheeks burn while I disentangle the last few brown strands from Alejandro's green ones, but I don't mind the guffaws. It's a welcome release from the tension of all the events that led us here.

I drop to my knees before Minnie. Her eyes show that she needs answers, but that she trusts me to give them to her. I stroke her cheek with the back of my fingers.

"Are you all right?" I ask softly.

"I don't know," she murmurs.

"Can you make it to the car?"

She nods and accepts my arm to stand.

"What about all of these people?" Wayne gestures to the group of Potestas members.

"Damn it. There are always loose ends." I run my hand through my hair in frustration. "I would love to press charges, but the whole situation is so complicated and out of any police officer's ballpark that I'm afraid it would be futile. Not to mention March probably has the best lawyers in the city. Granted, I can afford them if we need to, but it would be a battle."

"What if you change their memories?" Wayne says.

"Messing with their heads? I didn't think you would be up for that, Wayne," I say.

"I think it's justified in this case," he says firmly.

"I can do it, but a change that large will leave scars. They'll lose a piece of their lives that they'll never get back. If the process doesn't physically damage their minds, the psychological trauma of the lost time will cause issues. Personally, I think they've earned some trauma, but I'm open to hearing objections. Anyone?"

My friends are silent. The Potestas members who overheard my explanation start to shout, but I ignore them.

"Minnie, is that all right with you?" I say. "If I modify their memories so they have no recollection of needing to hurt you, this mad organization, any of it? Or would you like to press charges?"

"Can you really do that?" she says in a wandering voice. It was probably too much to ask her to make that decision, given what she's been through, but it really is hers to make.

"Yes," I say gently.

"Then do it. I don't want to think about this whole mess ever again."

"Alejandro?" I say. "Can you help Minnie through the tunnel? I'll catch you up shortly with this lot in tow. I suppose we shouldn't leave them here to be trapped by the tide."

Wayne's eyes widen.

"We should hurry. It's rising. Who knows how long we have?"

Wayne leads the way to the tunnel, and the rest of my friends file out of the cavern. One by one, I twist the strands of the Potestas members. Most look terrified and squirm incessantly, shouting obscenities and threats, at least until I knot the appropriate threads. Then a look of dreamy unconcern passes across their faces. I backhand each one on the cheek for good measure before I untie each. They don't deserve to walk away from this entirely unscathed. They take the punishment with composure in their trance-like states.

I approach Anna last. She alone has remained quiet during the process.

"What I wouldn't give to know your secrets," she says with a shake of her head. "So much potential, squandered."

"What makes you think I've squandered it?" I ask with real curiosity.

"Living as an underpaid instructor in a crummy apartment? I could do so much better with your opportunities."

"Oh, Anna. There's so much you don't know. I've lived in palaces, swum in the clearest lagoons, eaten gold-coated confectionaries, slept with the most divine women, sailed in the ships of kings. Trust me, I've plumbed the depths of my abilities." Recent revelations aside. "But, as trite as it sounds, it didn't bring me satisfaction, happiness, or peace. Not lasting, in any event. So, don't pine over what you will never have." I reach to her head and she winces. "Don't fret, I won't let you pine. In fact, you won't remember me, or Potestas, or spirits, ever again."

A tear traces down her cheek.

"Goodbye, Merry."

I gaze into her eyes before I tie the final knot.

"I hope you find what you're looking for, Anna."

Anna's tear-filled, passionate eyes glaze over. She gazes at me without recognition or concern. I rip the duct tape off her arms and legs and look around at my handiwork. A couple dozen former Potestas members stare blankly at the rocky walls. I clap my hands three times.

"Everyone, follow me. Let's leave this hole."

The members turn slowly, as if in a dream, and meander toward me. I shake my head and follow my friends into the light of a beautiful day. Minnie is waiting.

CHAPTER XXVI

I catch up with the group before they reach the wet part of the tunnel. A sloshing sound alerts me to danger.

"Hurry up, folks. The tide is rising."

I take over Alejandro's role in helping Minnie. The members traipse silently behind us, and my friends glance at them with consternation.

"Super creepy, Merry," Jen says to me quietly.

I would answer, but when we limp around a corner, light is visible at the end of the tunnel. It's now a third full of cold salt water, and waves surge toward us through the narrow opening. We charge ahead, hampered by the water. I glance at Minnie, whose face is pale but determined.

We burst forth into blazing light that nearly blinds us in its intensity. A strangled cry greets my ears.

"You're finally here!"

Cecil has dragged himself onto a rock. His face is bloodless from pain. My fix must have worn off. I pass Minnie once more to Alejandro and slosh over to Cecil.

"I can't do much with the tide rising," I say. "A few tweaks for the pain, then Wayne will have to carry you out of the water."

"Whatever," he gasps. "Just get me out of here."

I fiddle with the lauvan near his head, and he relaxes as I block the discomfort. Wayne carefully drapes Cecil over his back in a fireman's carry, and we rush out of the bay.

Around the corner, the waves are even worse. I keep Minnie upright, and Liam holds Wayne steady against the rising surges. The Potestas members press forward without emotion. It's a long, cold slog back to the car, and by the end we push through saltwater that is up to our waists.

185

At the cars, I siphon water off everyone, settle Minnie in my passenger's seat, and spend five minutes hastily healing Cecil.

"I'll fix you better tomorrow. Anyone need healing? Step up now."

Wayne pushes Gary forward, who grumbles but doesn't resist my attention. I fix his bruised jaw, Wayne's cracked ribs, Alejandro's sprained wrist, and Liam's bruised kidneys.

"What about them?" Wayne points at the Potestas members, who stand in a cluster at the edge of the parking lot.

"Don't worry about them. They'll wake up from their trance in a few hours. They'll be competent enough then. Can we meet up tomorrow to talk about all this?" I say with a thumb pointed at Minnie. "I want to take her home."

"Of course, Merlo," says Alejandro. The others nod in agreement. "Take care of Minnie."

I glance sideways as I turn the doorknob of my apartment. Minnie's eyes are fixed on my face and she is pale, too pale. Her midnight-blue lauvan cling tightly to her body so there is almost no separation between them and her physical form.

"Come on," I say. "Let's get you inside."

Minnie nods silently and steps past me when I hold the door open for her. She stops and hugs herself, as if she is unsure what to do next. I move to her and wrap my arms around her from the side. She stiffens briefly then turns to drop her head on my shoulder. I rub her back through the layers of her shirt and my coat, up and down on repeat. She leans more heavily into me.

The feeling from the sacrifice room, the feelings I was able

186

to set aside for a while in the face of Minnie's distress, roar back with a vengeance. I want Minnie. I want her beside me every day. I want to wake up and see her face on the pillow next to me. I want to hear about her day at work, every day. I want to take her to my favorite places around the globe—the prettiest beach in Thailand, the most awe-inspiring view of the red rocks in Arizona, the best bakery in Paris—and I want to stay here in this tiny apartment forever clutching each other. I want to watch her body change through all the glorious transformations of womanhood, and I want to kiss her until her fears of ageing melt into never-forgotten pleasure. I want to bicker about trivial things, and I want to explore and debate the bigger ideas deep into the night. I want to tell her who I am, everything, with nothing hidden. I want Minnie Dilleck, from this moment until death inevitably parts us.

I can't deny it any longer. I'm in love, and I don't know how to fall out of love. What's more, I've reached the point where I don't want to, despite the knowledge of our parting one day, the inexorable march toward death and loneliness. I can't fight this anymore, no matter what happens in the future.

Minnie stirs in my arms and I realize I've been clutching her fiercely. I loosen my grip, and she looks up at me. Her eyes are expressive, as if she knows exactly what I'm feeling. We gaze at each other for a moment. I feel naked in front of her understanding gaze, and I don't mind in the slightest. She closes her eyelids briefly, as if they are too heavy for her.

"I want a shower, but it seems like way too much effort." She closes her eyes. "I'm so tired."

"Do you want help?" I bite my tongue as I wait for Minnie's answer. Now that I'm in love, now that Minnie is a woman who really matters to me, I'm afraid of being too cavalier, scaring her off or driving her away. She's too important now to take chances with.

Happily, her lips twitch in an amused fashion. It's brief, but I catch it. A solemn expression back on her face, she opens her eyes.

"Yes, please."

I keep my arm around Minnie's shoulder as I navigate her to the bathroom. It's tiny, but we manage to squeeze in. I release Minnie and turn to run the shower for hot water. Once I'm satisfied it's the perfect temperature, I turn around.

Minnie stands before me, entirely naked. She looks a little self-conscious, clearly aware of my eyes on her. I let my gaze travel down her body—she may be nervous, but I'm a man, not a saint—and find myself wanting Minnie even more. She wouldn't make the cut for a magazine—her hips and thighs are plumper than the modern ideal, and her breasts are smaller—but I'm not a modern man. Her nipples stiffen, and her breasts tighten as my eyes reach them, perhaps from a mixture of my gaze and the cool air. My breathing quickens slightly.

"I hope you realize how beautiful you are," I say. Minnie looks away from my eyes and pushes air through her lips in a little huff of a laugh as if denying my admiration, but her cheeks grow pink and her lauvan squirm. I step back and spread my arm toward the shower. Minnie steps toward it but stops and turns when she passes me. She hovers for a moment, searching my face, then reaches a hand up to cup my head and guide it to her lips.

She's nervous and unsure, yet she knows exactly what to do to stoke the fire. Or perhaps anything she does will do that to me. I'm in too deep to know the difference.

Minnie finishes the kiss and steps into the shower without a word. I watch her bottom jiggle as she climbs over the sill and an image of Josephine climbing into a bathtub springs unbidden to my mind. Somehow the memory doesn't feel disrespectful to Minnie, nor does this moment diminish what I had with Josephine.

Quickly I undress, leaning against the counter to pull off my socks and dropping everything in a heap on the floor. I push aside the curtain and step into the shower. Minnie stands with her back to me, entirely still, allowing the water to pour over her bowed head in an endless deluge. Her wet hair is plastered to her neck and drapes on either side of her face. She looks so tired and helpless that my heart clenches, and I want to embrace her, to never let Potestas or anyone else hurt her ever again.

"Minnie." She doesn't respond. I say again, "Minnie. Let's get you clean and into bed, okay?"

She nods slightly but doesn't move. I pick up the bar of soap and rub it between my hands. I pause for a moment, considering, then carefully run my soapy hand over her shoulder and down her arm.

Minnie doesn't react physically, but her lauvan immediately relax from their tight clustering near her body. I'm heartened by this reaction, that she not only feels comfortable around me after all the strangeness at the sacrifice room, but that my touch on her naked skin soothes her. I feel like we know each other much better than we really do.

When I reach her wrist, she twists her arm and raises it above her head with her elbow crooked. I take it as an invitation to continue and run my hand down her arm toward her torso. Her dark blue strands wave lazily at me, but I refrain from touching them yet. When I reach her underarm, she flinches, and I jolt my hand away in consternation.

"What is it?" Did I hurt her? Go too far?

"Sorry. It just tickled." She gives a small chuckle and I breathe out in relief. I lather my hand and return it to her side. Minnie's threads immediately wrap around my own and my

189

eyes close with the pleasure of connection. It feels so natural that I wonder briefly what took us so long. Correction—what took me so long.

I continue soaping her body, eventually running my slippery hands over her breasts, sliding over her stiff nipples but not stopping, soaping her stomach in slow circles until enough of her lauvan wrap around the strands of my hand and inexorably draw it down between her legs.

When we finally make it to the bedroom, our lovemaking is unhurried. I have the sense that we've done this before, and we are simply reacquainting ourselves. It's funny what love makes you feel. There's also no rush because we have years ahead of us. Why not take the time to enjoy each other?

She comes, and I come right after. Our bodies slow and then stop. I hang my head as I prop my body above Minnie's on my elbows. Our panting breaths mingle as we lay still with me inside her. We're so close together, just the way we should be. Unexpectedly, my eyes start to burn with unshed tears, and I bury my face into Minnie's neck. She strokes my hair gently.

"What's wrong?" she whispers in my ear.

"I just want to stay in you, with you, this close to you forever." My voice is muffled but she must hear me because she squeezes me tightly.

"I'm not going anywhere."

I just hold her closer. She will, one day. It's inevitable. But I don't need to dwell on that. We're here together, today. That's enough. It will have to be.

CHAPTER XXVII

Dreaming

Arthur pulls on his boots by the fire while Guinevere packs his saddlebag. Morgan and her forces have attacked Framric's settlement again, the home of Guinevere's people, and we had no warning. Arthur sent out riders early this morning to muster our forces to aid Framric, and fighters have been trickling in. We are due to leave shortly.

But not before I speak with Nimue.

"Where are you going?" Arthur calls out after me as I stride through the hall. "We're leaving soon."

"I'll catch you up. I won't be long." My words barely make it out of my mouth before I am out the door toward the sleeping chambers.

Nimue folds my spare shirt and slides it into a saddlebag when I enter my chamber. She looks up and smiles, although her eyes are sad.

"I didn't think you would have to leave so soon after I arrived," she says. "But I understand duty."

"Nimue, I need to say something. I—well, you make me—" This is far harder than I anticipated. My heart beats in an irregular fashion and my palms are damp. I growl with frustration at my inability to speak the words in my heart. I know many dialects, but this translation eludes me until Nimue slides her slender fingers into mine.

"What do you wish to say?" She looks at me with a teasing smile. "Come, now, I've never known you to be tongue-tied."

"I had grander plans for this moment," I say hoarsely. "A beautiful view, perhaps. A meadow of flowers. But if I don't say it now, when can I? There's never a good time, but it's always the right time."

"The right time for what?" she whispers.

"Nimue, I love you. More than I've loved anyone. I don't know that I truly knew what love between two souls was until I met you. And I wish for your hand in marriage." She gasps softly at that, but I plow ahead. Now that the words are coming, I can't stop them. "I don't know what marriage would mean for us. You are the Lady of the Lake, with the responsibilities that entails, and I would never wish to get in the way of your duties. I am not a normal man, and I can't forsake Arthur and his mission to bring peace to our lands. All I know is that I want you to know that I am yours, all of me, forever."

Nimue's eyes glisten with unshed tears.

"I care not how we make this work, only that we do. You are my heart, Merlin. I will never leave you."

Guinevere looks around with interest from her seat on a gray palfrey. The rain has finally stopped, and she has pushed back the hood of her cloak from her blond braids to see better. Her riding trousers are damp, as are mine, but it doesn't seem to bother her despite the cold.

"What a beautiful valley," she declares. "Wet, like freshly washed laundry. We will catch cold from the wet, but the view makes up for it."

I smile at her enthusiasm.

"You're in a good mood. Is it the view, or the fact that you will see Arthur tonight at the villa?"

She grins playfully.

"Can it be both?"

"Of course. Indeed, I am looking forward to a break from campaigning. Winter came late this year. It was a long series of battles this summer."

"And a long summer keeping Lady Lyn company, for me," says Guinevere. "It is nothing to fighting, but I will be glad to be in my own home. She is very…"

"Overbearing?" I say.

"Yes. But her house is safe in the hills, and I am grateful for her hospitality."

We ride with an escort of five fighting men and three of Guinevere's ladies. The horse of the frontmost rider whickers nervously. I look around with a frown. We are dipping into a crevasse between rocks as we descend into the valley, with thick bushes on either side. It is the perfect spot for an ambush.

As the thought occurs to me, an arrow lands with a thud in the thigh of one of the men. He screams. The crevasse erupts with neighing horses and panicked riders. Another arrow forces a fighter to the ground. While I slide my sword from my scabbard and prepare to dismount, something punches my shoulder with the force of two men. I am expelled from my saddle and land with a thump amid thundering hooves.

The pain comes next. Fire follows tearing pressure and rips through my flesh with unbearable heat. My focus is torn away from the pain by Guinevere's screams. I lumber to my feet, my vision tunneling briefly from the motion in my arrow wound.

I'm too late. The fight was over before it had truly begun. We were hopelessly overwhelmed, taken by surprise. Guilt churns my stomach at the sight of fellow fighters writhing on the ground and the women tightly contained in Saxon arms. Guinevere has a cut lip and her braids are coming undone, but she looks defiant. The Saxons laugh and look pleased with themselves while some rifle through our saddlebags for plunder.

A large Saxon strides forward. He is older and clearly did not take part in the skirmish, although I have no doubt that he would be a formidable foe. His dirty blond hair is slicked back in rows and his broad face looks familiar. I narrow my eyes and weigh my chances against these men. I am wounded and outnumbered, but how can I stand idle? As I make up my mind to attack, Guinevere gasps.

"Uncle?" she says breathlessly in Saxon. The large man peers at her. "Uncle, it's Guinevere, Framric's daughter. You must remember me."

"Little Vera?" The man's eyes widen. "So it is. What in Woden's name are you doing at the wrong end of a raiding party?" He waves at the Saxon holding Guinevere, and the man lets go. Guinevere rubs her arms.

"Father married me to the Briton Arthur, years ago now, to seal the truce. Father and his tribe live peacefully alongside the Britons now. When did you arrive from the mainland? Has my father not spoken of this? Why have you attacked us?" Her voice grows stronger with every question. Her uncle blinks.

"We are on our way to see your father. He invited us to settle with him. I lead a small party to assess. As for attacking you, I would never hurt little Vera. I thought you were a group of lowly Britons, ripe for plundering. A little gold never goes amiss."

Guinevere puts her hands on her hips.

"Uncle, I am glad to see you. But you must understand, these 'lowly Britons' are our friends and allies now. I suggest you refrain from any more raids until you speak with my father and understand who is friend and who is foe."

Her uncle gazes at her for a moment, either debating her advice or wondering when "little Vera" became a fierce woman. I hold my breath and try not to pass out from the fiery pain. Finally, he nods.

"Release them," he orders his men. They grumble but obey. Guinevere's women flock behind her, and the men who are

194

able drag themselves to their feet. The uncle walks forward and clasps Guinevere's hands between his own.

"Well met, my niece. My apologies for the attack. Can we aid your wounded?"

With a half-glance at me, Guinevere declines.

"Thank you, uncle, but we will manage. May we meet next time as friends."

CHAPTER XXVIII

I wake with a heart full of lightness. It's such an uncommon occurrence these days that the reason puzzles me. Why am I so happy?

I open my eyes and remember why. Minnie's head lies on my pillow. Her dark hair frames her face with a tendril over her forehead. Her bare shoulder is pale and fragile-looking, so I gently pull the blanket over her.

The slight movement wakes Minnie. Her eyes flutter open, and it takes her a moment to focus on my sheepish face. She smiles in question.

"Good morning. Why do you look so guilty?"

"I didn't mean to wake you. I was only fixing the covers."

She reaches out in response, and I fold her in an embrace. We rearrange our limbs until her back and bottom are nestled against my front.

We lie in this position, unspeaking, for several minutes. It's utterly blissful. A creeping veil of sadness, of the thought that this can't last, threatens to overwhelm the moment. I banish the feeling. What's the point of having such moments if I can't enjoy them? I made my choice.

"Are you going back to sleep?" Minnie whispers.

"No. This moment is too pleasant to waste on sleep. You?"

"I've had enough. Well, I could probably sleep for a week, but I've had enough to hear an explanation about yesterday."

"Ah, yes." I suppose it had to happen sooner rather than later. "Can I ask first, what did it look like on your end?"

Minnie lets out her breath in a long, contemplative sigh.

"I drove to Pacific Spirit Park at lunch yesterday, thinking there was a hiking group I was joining. A bunch of people were there, they were friendly enough but a little strange in retrospect. Odd glances, you know. We walked for maybe twenty minutes. We were nearing the other side, where the path gets close to the road, when they grabbed me, tied me up with a gag and a blindfold, and threw me in a van. We drove and drove, and when they finally took off the blindfold, I was in a gross old basement. They fed me, but no one spoke, not once. In the morning, they drove to Scotia Park and forced me into the tunnel at knifepoint."

I squeeze Minnie tightly.

"If I hadn't broken it off with you, I would have joined you at this so-called mountaineering club, and none of this would have happened."

Minnie rubs my arm. Her voice has a trace of a smile.

"We can't predict the future. Don't beat yourself up over it. Anyway, we finally made it to the central cave. They set up battery-powered lights, then drew a big circle on the ground and forced me to the center. I couldn't move after that, I don't know what they did. Then they held hands around the circle and chanted." She shivers. "It was really creepy. That's when I started getting even more worried, if that was possible. I'd learned enough about cults in my studies to see the signs. There was a flash of color, just for a moment, then it was silent. They were still chanting, but I couldn't hear it. There was nothing I could do but wait to die."

She stops for a moment, and her shoulders tremble. I clutch her tightly, disgusted with Potestas, with myself for being too slow.

"But then, you and your friends turned up," she says. Her voice is surprisingly strong. "It was pretty amazing to see. The cult was falling like flies under your attack. And your faces—you all meant business. I've never felt such a wave of pure gratitude and hope as I did then.

"Then you called Alejandro over and waved your hands

around, and you went all strange. You walked like you were newly blind, carefully and stiff-legged. And there was nothing behind your eyes. I would have been terrified had it been anyone but you.

"And that's it. I must have passed out, because when I woke up, the fight was over."

Minnie wriggles in my arms until we are face to face.

"So? How did you find me? What was the cult about? And what happened to you in that circle?"

I stare into her blue eyes, scarcely covered by lauvan now. Looks like it's time, whether I'm ready or not. Perhaps I should shout it out from my balcony—my powers are hardly a secret, now.

"The cult, as you put it, is called Potestas."

I briefly outline the organization and what they were attempting to do. Minnie's eyebrows rise in incredulity with the mention of spirits, but after a moment I can tell she remembers the strange abilities of the Potestas members, and her skepticism wavers.

"Wait, those voices you were hearing. That wasn't a mental health issue, was it?"

"No, that was me hearing spirits. Hence, why I didn't follow up with the psychiatrist you referred me to. I'm certain that medication wouldn't have helped, in this case."

"And how did you become a member in this organization?" Minnie asks. "Do you have a crystal ball I should know about?"

"Not quite. There's a complicated story about a volcano—"

Minnie's face clears in understanding.

"Wallerton. You've mentioned it before."

During our therapy sessions, I told her about it in relation to my intimacy with Anna. I hastily move on.

"But they found out then that I have abilities that they both

198

envy and covet. They invited me in to use me how they could, and I accepted to bring them down from the inside."

"Abilities?" Minnie's expression is curious and expectant. My lip twitches in a growing grin. I reach over and grab the waving lauvan from a water glass on the bedside table.

"Open your mouth," I instruct and slowly guide a large droplet of water through the air. It gently lands in Minnie's awestruck open mouth. She swallows then blinks at me.

"Was that for real?" She shakes her head in disbelief. "Is it an elaborate trick, or magic?"

"Magic, you could call it." I search her face for signs of fear. She pulls me closer.

"That's sexy," she breathes in my ear. "Stop trying to turn me on when I have more questions. There will be plenty of time for magic later."

I laugh in delight. That is possibly the best reaction I could ever hope for. I reach under the sheet and grab her hip to press into mine while I kiss her. She pulls away after a sweet minute of caressing and pulls the sheet up in a show of modesty.

"Be good, Dr. Lytton," she chastises me with a wink. "Now what are these abilities?"

I flop onto my back in defeat.

"There is an aura—for lack of a better word—around everything with energy. I can see it, touch it, move it, and change the physical world with it."

"Huh." She gazes at me for a moment. "And how did that happen? Nuclear accident? Deal with the devil?"

"I was born with it." I pause and my brow furrows. "Actually, I just found out. My mother was human, but my father, apparently, was a spirit. Earth elemental to be precise. So, that makes me…" I stare at the ceiling. "I don't know what that makes me."

"What emotions are stirred by this discovery?" Minnie has

her professional voice on, which makes me smile and look at her. She smiles back, aware of my noticing but undeterred.

"I don't know. Anger, I suppose, that he was alive until recently and never sought me out. But, then, he was in a different plane of existence." I grind the heel of my palm against my forehead in frustration. "Regret that I might have had an opportunity to find out more about myself. More anger that the information would have come at the cost of your life. Guilt that a tiny part of me still wanted to know. Confusion. What am I? What do I do with this knowledge?"

Minnie nods slowly, then lays a hand on my chest.

"For what it's worth, you have my forgiveness for wanting to know." She strokes my chest with soft fingers. "And I don't know what it means for you. I hardly know what to think of all this. But I do know that I want to figure it out with you." She leans over and kisses me on the shoulder, neck, jaw. She stops with her lips almost touching mine. "Together?"

"Together," I agree, and wrap my arms around her waist. I had debated telling her about my lengthy past right now, since she is taking this all so well, but it can wait. We have more important things to do first.

I was afraid that Minnie would be fearful after her kidnapping experience, but her trust in me is absolute that I have stopped Potestas for good. She is relaxed and, despite a little fatigue, in good health.

"I need to go home, get clean clothes," she says. "I'll cancel my appointments today, though. I think a mental health day is in order after almost being killed." She smiles at me while she buttons her shirt to let me know she's all right. "Tea and a good

200

book are what I'll prescribe to myself."

I try to smile, but it twists on my mouth. I don't want her to go, not now that I've finally admitted my love for her to myself. I don't want to appear overly insecure, so I don't voice my thoughts aloud. They must be written on my face, for Minnie laughs lightly and bends down to plant a kiss on my lips.

"I'll be back tonight, if you'll have me."

"I suppose I'll have to be satisfied to be your booty call," I say. I pull Minnie to the bed and press the length of my body against hers while I kiss her. When I release her, her cheeks are flushed and her eyes bright. I stand and pull her up. "Just to make sure you come back."

"Unnecessary, but not unwelcome." She kisses me on the cheek then walks out the door. I watch her go with a foolish grin on my face.

Then I remember that I'm fully naked, and Alejandro will come over soon. I need to tell him about my heritage revelations, and since he and Jen don't seem to be talking yet, I can't rely on her to keep him informed.

When there is a knock on the door, I am dressed and filling the kettle in the kitchen.

"Come in," I call out. Alejandro walks into the kitchen with a pensive expression, but his brow furrows when he looks around.

"I thought Minnie would be here."

"She just left." I pull mugs from the cupboard.

"So, you two are together now?"

I sigh, in both happiness and resignation.

"It appears so. I have bowed to the inevitable." I look at Alejandro. He is lost in thought once more. "What has you so reflective?"

"It's these dreams." He rubs his temples. "They're getting

201

stronger. I didn't say anything while we were looking for Minnie—too much going on—but sometimes even in the day I get visions." He stares at me with confused panic simmering below the surface. "Merlo, do you believe in reincarnation?"

"You're not the first person to ask me that recently. Anna Green said something similar." Alejandro's hands tremble, so I steer him by the shoulder to sit on a dining room chair. "Go on, tell me what you think is happening."

"Every night, endless dreams. I'm always me, but in different times and places. And yesterday, when we were fighting Potestas, I had visions of me fighting alongside others. And you, always you, in most of these dreams." Alejandro rubs his face, but it doesn't appear to bring him any clarity. "It's been ever since I touched the grail. Am I going crazy? Or…"

"Or what?"

"Or is it possible that I used to be Arthur?"

I simply stare at him. My first thought is of denial. I've never heard of such a thing, so how could it be true? Then I remember my recent introduction to the spirits, and my conviction wavers. Is Alejandro's theory so far-fetched? The reaction he had with the grail—something fundamental happened, I'm sure. March and Anna's knowing looks suddenly make more sense when viewed through this lens. Do they also know me from my past? From our shared past?

Then my brain catches up. If what Alejandro says is true, then Arthur has returned, in a fashion. He honored his promise.

I'm alone no longer.

"It sounds ridiculous out loud," says Alejandro. "That I'm claiming to be some ancient king. Conceited. If reincarnation is real, then it's more likely that I was some muddy peasant. But, these dreams." He closes his eyes briefly. "They're so real, so much detail. How could I imagine them? They feel like memories, not dreams."

My dreams are memories, also, so I know what Alejandro means. My mouth opens, but no words spill out. I clear my throat and try again.

"Tell me about a dream that I'm not in," I say hoarsely. "I need to know you're not simply viewing my own visions, that somehow transferred to you."

Alejandro nods and closes his eyes. His voice grows less strained and more wandering.

"I am in a room with a large fireplace, benches, tapestries on the walls. It feels like home. I am dirty and tired, but happy. A woman kisses me. She is tall, blond, beautiful—I say her name, Guinevere. I give her a bundle wrapped in coarse cloth. When she opens it, there is a folded pile of golden-yellow fabric, embroidered at the edge with tiny white flowers. Guinevere is very happy, she promises to make a dress for Lúnasa." Alejandro stumbles on the word, as if it is foreign on his tongue. He opens his eyes and looks at me with a mute question.

"I always wondered where she had received that dress," I say with wonder. "She said it was a gift from a dragon, then laughed."

"I bought it from a peddler we met on the road to Gwent, after a skirmish in Ergyng," Alejandro says with easy assurance, as if it is a sentence he often says. Then his eyes widen.

My breath comes faster and faster. Fifteen centuries I've waited, never finding what I've searched for. Can Arthur truly have returned? Why now?

"Wait, you said you remember different times and places," I say with urgency. "Who else do you remember being?"

"Men named Alexios, Abelin, Axel," Alejandro says with confidence. "Without knowing more history, or dreaming more, I couldn't give you dates. Abelin may have been from

203

World War Two."

I'm hyperventilating now. Arthur, Arthur has been by my side for all these years, and I've never known. He's come back, again and again, just as he said he would. My life's purpose, as frail and hopeless and ridiculous as it may have seemed, has been answered.

"You, you—" My words choke me, and I start babbling in Brythonic, my native tongue. "It's you, it's always been you. You said you would come, you did, and you were right. How could I not have seen it? How could I have been so blind?"

Alejandro looks at me with narrowed eyes and a tilted head.

"I understand some of the words, but I don't know what language you're speaking. But, Merlo, tell me, is it true?"

I grip my hair, unable to control my breathing.

"I don't understand how, but yes, somehow, yes."

We stare at each other for a long moment. Alejandro's brown eyes look at me out of a very different face from Arthur's, and yet the expression is one I recognize, and I fancy I can see Arthur looking out of Alejandro's eyes. Alejandro's lauvan swirl in slow circles, confused yet hopeful. They are a dark, forest green, unlike Arthur's vibrant spring green. And yet, as I think back to the men whose names Alejandro mentioned, all of them had green lauvan, in progressively darker shades through the ages. It's one more piece of evidence that he is really Arthur.

I spread my arms and encircle Alejandro in a fierce hug. I don't know if he can feel all the years of loss and hope in the action, but his returning embrace is firm and unwavering.

A knock at the door breaks the moment. I turn moist eyes to the hallway where Jen stands with an unsure expression.

"Is this a bad time? I can come back," she says to me.

"No, no, it's…" My voice trails off as I stare at Jen's golden lauvan. If they were paler, they would be the color of wheat.

Long ago, I knew a woman with strands like that.

"Your strange dreams—when did they start?" I ask in a strangled voice. I point at the grail on the coffee table. "Did you ever touch the grail?"

Jen looks taken aback.

"How did you—yes, I was going to mention it when things settled down. I had a look at it when you brought it back from the boat, before you buried it and it was stolen."

"Did you have a strange reaction?"

"I guess so," she says, her eyes gazing at me in confusion. "I felt tingly, and I came over faint. I might have blacked out for a moment. Then I was fine, and I didn't notice anything else, otherwise I would have said something. But that night, the dreams started."

"Merlo," says Alejandro with wide eyes. "Who do you think she is?"

I keep my eyes on Jen.

"Have you been dreaming that you're Guinevere?"

Jen visibly starts, her eyes round.

"Yes," she whispers. "What does it mean?"

I look at Alejandro, who gazes at Jen with a look of angst and awe.

"Jen." I swallow, then compose myself. "Do you believe in reincarnation?"

CHAPTER XXIX

Jen stares at me, her eyes as round as Alejandro's.

"Are you saying," she stammers. "You think—I was Guinevere in a past life? The Guinevere you knew?"

I let out a strangled cry and bury my face in my hands. This is too much. How is this possible? I don't know how to bear such hope, such pain, such happiness, such regret. It's too much.

Jen waits for an answer, so I lift my head out of my hands.

"I think, yes. Somehow." I stand and raise my hand to her cheek. She gazes at me, and I speak to her in slow Saxon. "Guinevere, my dear, do you remember me?"

It takes a moment, then recognition flickers in Jen's eyes and she inhales sharply. Then she replies in halting Saxon, and it brings me a painful delight so strong I can barely breathe.

"I'm starting to, Merlin. I don't know how, but I do."

I wrap her in a crushing embrace and squeeze my eyes shut tightly. I am overcome.

When I finally let go, Jen's eyes are wet, and she dashes them away with the back of her fingers with a moist chuckle.

"I lived a quiet life before you, Merry," she says in English. "Since I met you, I've had more changes to my world philosophy than anyone should. Magic, immortality, spirits, and now—" She swallows with a half-fearful, half-laughing look. "Past lives? And of one of the most famous women of legend? I don't even know what to think."

"I don't know, either," I say. I'm still breathing too fast. "Everything is just—" I exhale. "I need some air. Give me a minute."

I slide open the balcony door and lean over the railing. A stiff breeze passes through my hair in a welcome ruffle and I close my eyes to simply feel. My brain turns off, and I let emotions flush and fade through my body.

Alejandro's quiet voice drifts through the open door. He's clearly trying to avoid my hearing him, but I have keen ears.

"Jen? I want to say I'm sorry. For what I said to you the other day."

"Are we going to ignore the whole past-lives elephant in the room?" Jen's voice is hard, tinged with exasperation.

"Just for a minute. I took what you said, and my mind twisted it into something that you didn't mean. Just because I was grieving my uncle, doesn't mean I could lash out at you."

"No, it doesn't," Jen says, then she sighs. "Thanks, Alejandro. Apology accepted."

There is a long pause.

"Where does that leave us?" Alejandro says finally. "These dreams, our past. Are we destined to be together?"

"I don't care what was in my past," Jen says. "I have to live the life I have now. You hurt me, we broke up, and now I'm dating Cecil. Whatever might have happened a thousand years ago, this is our reality now."

That sounds final. I doubt Alejandro has much to say in response, so I turn and walk inside. They sit on either end of the couch. Outwardly, they look ill-at-ease, but the lauvan that join them together are still strong. The deep gold and dark green entwined together are like a shadowed echo of their bond so many centuries ago. How could I have not seen it? How would I have known to look?

"Why, Merry?" says Jen. "Do you know how, why this happened? Does everyone have a past life, or is it just us? What—" She grinds the heels of her hands against her temples as if a migraine builds there.

"I don't know." I spread my hands and shrug. "I truly know nothing. This is the first time in fifteen hundred years—" I choke when I think of the centuries of loneliness that never really were. "That I've had even the slightest inkling of this."

My stomach asserts itself, and I'm reminded how hungry I am and how empty my fridge is. Even during insane, life-altering revelations, the body has needs.

"We have more to speak of, but I need fuel. I'll grab something from the café downstairs."

"I'll come with you," says Alejandro, clearly not ready to be alone again with his former girlfriend. Wife? Even I'm confused.

"I'll make some coffee here," Jen says quickly. Her hands tremble, and I wonder if coffee is really the beverage she needs right now. It gives her something concrete to do and concentrate on, though, so I nod. Alejandro follows me out the door.

We're quiet in the elevator down, each of us too lost in our own thoughts to say much to the other. There is so much I want to say to Arthur, to Alexios, to Abelin, but Alejandro is not these men, not entirely. His essence is the same, but their lives are only memories to him. Perhaps that will change with time. Perhaps, as Alejandro remembers more and more, he will meld with the others to become an amalgam of all the friends I've had before. I hope so. I look forward to it.

"What does this mean?" Alejandro asks as we walk to the café. "For me, for us, for our lives going forward?"

"I have no idea." I look at him and give a half-smile. "Shall we find out together?"

His returning grin is infectious.

We return to my floor of the apartment building laden with

sandwiches and pastries. Jen meets us at the door. Her eyes are wide, and she holds her clenched fist over her mouth.

"Merry, Minnie came back, she forgot her phone. Then she touched the grail."

Jen's eyes are full of unshed tears, and my heart plummets to my stomach.

"What happened? Is she all right?" I push past Jen with fear in my heart.

"No, no, she's fine, its—"

Jen doesn't finish her sentence. I burst into the living room and stop. Minnie sits on the end of the couch. My sketchbook is on her lap, open to a central page with a tempera painting of Zanetta, my twelfth wife I met in Venice. Minnie glances at me briefly with a welcoming smile then looks back to the picture.

"I can't believe you drew me in this terrible dress. I hated red—I only wore it when my stepmother visited, since she had given me the fabric as a wedding present." Minnie chuckles and flips a few pages to Isabella of eleventh century Spain, my sixth wife. "Oh, yes, al-Andalus. Do you remember buying almonds in the market and eating them on the banks of the river? We used to share them with that urchin child who lived nearby. You gave her your coat once, I recall."

I can only stare at Minnie's face, which is content and tranquil. I am anything but. My mind has ground to a halt. I can't think, can't breathe, can't see anything but Minnie flipping the pages of my memories.

There is no way she could know what she says. No way unless—the grail. She touched the grail. Could—could she—my mind can't take these revelations, and my breathing starts again in heaving gasps. Minnie turns back to the first page. Arthur, Guinevere, Elian, Gawaine, Gareth are all there, in the blocky artistry of the fifth century. Minnie's fingers brush over the larger figure of Nimue on the bottom right. Then she looks at me with a smile sweeter than the clearest honey.

"Merlin, my love," she whispers in Brythonic, the language of my birth. "You should have known I would never leave you."

I choke on the rising sob in my throat. I'm on my knees without any recollection of dropping. I'm weighed down, pressed by a force far greater than gravity, by the knowledge of so many wasted years, so much regret and sorrow and loss, when all along I've never been left. My eyes close, and sobs wrack my body. Nimue. It's always been Nimue. The only thought that keeps me from sinking to the floor entirely is that I am reunited with Nimue once more, my only love. Every love I've found through all my long years has been me reacquainting myself with her. I weep for the years of grief, of endless sorrows that have piled up on me over the centuries. Every time I lost a love to the ravages of time that I never feel myself, I thought she was gone forever. Every time I found someone new, I had to banish the lingering guilt of moving on.

So much emotion, entirely needless. And now, too much emotion overwhelms me.

My eyes are closed, but I can feel Minnie kneel before me. Dimly, I hear the front door close. Alejandro and Jen must have left to give us this moment alone. Minnie's gentle hands cup my head and caress my neck. I rest my head on her shoulder and let my tears soak her shirt.

When my sobs dwindle to shuddering breaths, I raise my head. Minnie's hand moves from the back of my head to my cheek. She wipes the wetness away with tender fingers. Her clear blue eyes meet mine.

"It's always been you," I whisper. She nods.

"Always. I couldn't let you do this on your own."

"You came back, on purpose? You chose this?"

She frowns in thought.

"No, I don't know how this works, nor why I keep coming back to you. But I know that if I could have chosen, I would have done the same thing."

I lean into her hand on my cheek.

"I would like to know how it all works," she says. Her eyes crinkle in a smile. "Shall we find out together?"

"Yes," I whisper. "Together. Always."

CHAPTER XXX

Dreaming

The boat rocks slightly as Gretchen touches her hand to my cheek. We lie in the bottom of my tiny fishing vessel, our heads together and our feet at opposite ends. The lake is placid today, and fluffy white clouds drift in a lazy current through the blue above. Gretchen's blond hair tickles my neck, and she rubs her rounded belly.

"I think it will be a boy," she says. "Perhaps. I don't know how other women can tell. Can you see, Marian, with the strands?"

"No, more's the pity. We'll have to wait like every other new parent." I turn in a quest for her lips, and she rewards me with a kiss.

"I can't wait," she says after our lips part. "I suppose it will be short for you, but months is a long time for me."

"Time stretches and shortens as it sees fit. It will be a long wait for me, too."

"So much time," she muses. Her elbow props up her head, so she can look at my face. Her expression is mischievous. "You know what I would love?"

"Are you craving liver again?"

"No. I would love to break bread with your former wives. It would be too much fun to speak with them, hear their take on you." She laughs in delight, and I give a playful shudder.

"That sounds like my nightmare."

She strokes a lock of hair off my forehead, a smile lingering on her full-lipped mouth.

"We all have something in common, so that's a start. We all love you."

"You're right. You do have things in common. Deep

loyalty, playful whimsy, and a pure and beautiful soul shining through your eyes." I trace my fingers around Gretchen's right eye, pondering the similarities between Gretchen and my previous eight wives. "I suppose I can't help but be drawn to that."

"Perhaps you were drawn to each of us. Perhaps it was all meant to be."

"I stopped believing in fate centuries ago." I smile to soften my words, but Gretchen looks thoughtful.

"Perhaps you simply can't see the whole picture. If you keep walking your path, your purpose will be made clear."

I exhale sharply.

"How long must I walk to understand that?"

"No one can know their path." She leans over to kiss my nose lightly. "Have faith."

CHAPTER XXXI

It's almost painful to leave Minnie now that I know who she really is, but she insisted on checking in at work, so I'm on my own for a few hours. I pull up my car in front of Sweet Thing. I need to find out if March is still there, what happened to the other members whose memories I didn't mess with. I need to know they are shut down for good.

It's midday, so cupcake sales are in full swing. I go straight to the washroom, and when I emerge, my shirt is the same color as the employees. When their attention is on customers, I slide behind the counter. If they spot me in their peripheral vision, they will assume I am one of them.

The door to Potestas opens easily, and I enter. The door clicks behind me.

The place is cleared out. No couches in the common area, no chairs in the meeting room, even the fridge is gone from the kitchen. Gone is the convivial atmosphere of this strange, cultish club, and the only things left are dust and darkness. I stride to the library, the room of reflection, the amulet acquisition room, but all are empty. In March's office, there is nothing but a folded notecard. I pick it up with foreboding in my heart.

Merry Lytton,

You'll be happy to know Potestas is disbanded, and its members gone their separate ways. I hope you are satisfied. It's not enough for you to have almost limitless powers—I suppose it's natural to want to be the only bully in the playground. Know that I will keep searching for the spirits, and I hope I will have the courtesy to share the wealth with others, courtesy that you have always lacked. Until we meet again,

March Feynman

A chill runs over me. What does she mean, courtesy that I have always lacked? She's known me for a few weeks, at most.

But, she touched the grail. Is March also someone from my past?

It doesn't matter now. She has disappeared. The more important people from my past are here and by my side. I can ignore cryptic messages, to be deciphered another day. Now, my long-lost, always found love is waiting for me. I will go find her, as I always have.

I am not alone.

ALSO BY EMMA SHELFORD

Immortal Merlin
Ignition
Winded
Floodgates
Buried
Possessed
Unleashed
Worshiped
Unraveled

Magical Morgan
Daughters of Dusk

Nautilus Legends
Free Dive
Caught
Surfacing

Breenan Series
Mark of the Breenan
Garden of Last Hope
Realm of the Forgotten

ACKNOWLEDGEMENTS

Many thanks to my tireless editors, Gillian and Guy Brownlee and Wendy and Chris Callendar. Deranged Doctor Designs produced another compelling cover. Amanda Wells kindly provided me with inspiration for a dreaming chapter. And, last but not least, Steven Shelford gave his input, patience, and support.

ABOUT THE AUTHOR

Emma Shelford feels that life is only complete with healthy doses of magic, history, and science. Since these aren't often found in the same place, she created her own worlds where they happily coexist. If you catch her in person, she will eagerly discuss Lord of the Rings ad nauseam, why the ancient Sumerians are so cool, and the important role of phytoplankton in the ocean.

Emma is the author of the Nautilus Legends (a marine biologist discovers that mythical sea creatures are real), Immortal Merlin (Merlin is immortal, forever young, and living in the modern day), and the Breenan Series (a young woman follows a mysterious stranger into an enchanting Otherworld).

Printed in Great Britain
by Amazon